PRAISE for THE POLISH COMPLEX

Chicago Tribune—

"The publication of *The Polish Complex* in the U.S. is a particularly important event. . . . It is a blunt and angry complaint about conditions in Konwicki's homeland, and about the injustice of a world in which Soviets reign supreme while Poles go wanting. It is also at times a comedy of manners, a biography of the author, a confession of bad faith, a philosophical treatise on good and evil, a history of the misguided Polish romantic spirit, and an urgent warning to the West."

New York Times Book Review—

"An impassioned, furious polemic on Poland's impossible condition. Konwicki . . . writes like a man who has nothing to lose—and who wants to use that freedom for the primary and urgent task of speaking the raw, unmediated truth."

John Updike, *New Yorker*—

"Like such other anarchic spirits as Flann O'Brien and Céline, Konwicki has a lovely way of writing, which never clogs chaos with self-pity and bestows upon the direst pages sentences of casual magic. . . . Konwicki is effortlessly witty."

Library Journal—

"[*The Polish Complex*] offers an incisive vision of Poland's history and national psyche. . . . A poignant dichotomy emerges as the book's central theme: Poland's past was violent and tragic (as shown by two digressions into the failed 1863 rebellion) but it offered the individual the chance for heroic behavior. The translator does well by this witty, sardonic work, which is highly recommended."

Washington Post Book World —

"Allows us to enter the life of Poland and experience its absurdities and contradictions. Through [it] we view the world from inside the collapsing human pyramid."

New Republic —

"Voices like Konwicki's should be listened to today with special attention."

Best Sellers —

"The whole story is like a phantom. . . . The movements in and out of the fictional reality to the narrator's fantasy are like the movements in a Tudor ballet. . . . While one waits in line, one converses, dreams, and has a coronary; these too are part of the metaphor, part of the complex. The complex is history, is being caught between Orthodox-Communist Russia and Lutheran-Communist Germany; so Roman Catholicism takes on not only a religious role, but a social-political role, making language-custom-religion-history part of oneself as the country slips, politically, from one emperor to the next."

World Literature Today —

"The novel's main leitmotiv depicts, in turgid prose, an eternally dark, cosmic landscape marred by the excrescences of modern civilization, a faithless world lacking in moral fiber but rich in banality."

Voice Literary Supplement —

"Bitterly funny."

THE POLISH COMPLEX

by TADEUSZ KONWICKI

TRANSLATED by RICHARD LOURIE

DALKEY ARCHIVE PRESS

Library of Congress Cataloging-in-Publication Data:

Konwicki, Tadeusz.
        [Kompleks polski. English]
        The Polish complex : a novel / by Tadeusz Konwicki ; translated by
Richard Lourie. — 1st Dalkey Archive ed.
                p.   cm.
        ISBN 1-56478-201-8 (pbk. : alk. paper)
        I. Lourie, Richard, 1940–   II. Title.
PG7158.K6513K613   1998
891.8'537373—dc21   98-23365
                                                          CIP

This publication is partially supported by grants from the National
Endowment for the Arts, a federal agency, and the Illinois Arts Council, a
state agency.

Dalkey Archive Press
Illinois State University
Campus Box 4241
Normal, IL 61790-4241

visit our website at: www.cas.ilstu.edu/english/dalkey/dalkey.html

TRANSLATOR'S INTRODUCTION

Konwicki's book describes a complex of which it is itself a part and product. The typically human act of
trying to see oneself is always fascinating, agonizing,
comical, for we can never turn fast enough to see all
sides at once in the mirror. And the greatest trick remains seeing how we see.

As a formation the Polish complex is a trinity, a
force manifested in three sets of relationships: Poland–
Russia, Poland–the West, and Poland–itself. It would,
however, be a serious error to conclude that this complex, though thoroughly historical, is limited to the fate
and personalities of nations. Though it is true to say
that Polish history created the Polish complex, it is, of
course, equally true to say the opposite. Truer still would
be to say that both processes occur simultaneously, like
some subatomic rarities which are never present alone.

The three aspects of the complex are so essentially

integrated that it is nearly impossible to speak of them separately. To approach them through historical details would require a strenuous expedition; Polish history is a dark and misleading woods. So, if the history of Poland were reduced to a fable it would tell of a strong, free kingdom surrounded by greedy neighbors ruled by cruel kings. But the people of the good kingdom did not wish to concern themselves with their neighbors' plans; they preferred to do as they pleased, for that was freedom. Then the armies came and took away the kingdom's freedom, and none of the countries that were supposed to be friends did anything to help.

This is a tragic history in the true Aristotelian sense. But, just as the Classical Age was succeeded by the Christian era, so tragedy can be overcome by resurrection. Poland in its darkest century was identified by its romantic poets as the Christ of nations. The term evoked both the fact of crucifixion and the promise of rebirth. The Polish imagination felt itself summoned both to the unpleasant cunning of survival and to exalted martyrdom.

Poland lost its freedom. It was erased from the map of Europe at the end of the eighteenth century and did not reappear until after the First World War. It rose twice against its oppressors in rebellions that partook of both glory and vainglory, according to a familiar recipe. Konwicki, in his two lengthy historical digressions, identifies with those rebellions, particularly that of 1863. If the history of the world is the record of freedom, freedom lost and freedom sought again, Poland is the paradigm of that process. What maddens Konwicki is that the paradigm is illegible, or untranslatable, or simply one too shocking to consider. Konwicki raises other embarrassing matters— justice, the nature of the world and our life in it. Why is evil triumphant, why is good weak? Or, to phrase the question in historical terms, why does Russia thrive and Poland suffer captivity and desecration?

It can be said that Poland was resurrected, but it was a shoddy, ersatz, twentieth-century resurrection and there was a terrific hangover. No one has it worse than Konwicki.

Richard Lourie

THE POLISH COMPLEX

I was standing in line in front of a state-owned jewelry store. I was twenty-third in line. In a short while the chimes of Warsaw would announce that it was eleven o'clock in the morning. Then the locks on the great glass and metal doors would rattle open and we, the sneezing and sniffling customers, would invade the store's elegant interior—though, of course, ours would be a well-disciplined invasion, each person keeping the place staked out during the long wait in line.

It was the day before Christmas, fairly cold, something between a late autumn day and one late in winter. There was a belated feeling about the day itself as well. Not fully illuminated, misty, sluggish. Stray snowflakes sailed through the icy air like poplar seeds. The tram cars huddled in herds on the broad trunk line, their bells clanging plaintively. A beggar familiar to all Warsaw sat himself down on the sidewalk near the jewelry store. He spread out his legs in the light, shifting snow to intimidate fainthearted passersby. But I knew that his prostheses, made of plastic and nickel, were hollow, and though they might freeze to the sidewalk, our beggar would feel no cold. Endless crowds of pedestrians rushed by along the walls. Occasionally one, lost in thought, would collide with another, yet would keep on walking without apology. Or one would jostle another with a Christmas tree, then curse him out. Some stumbled and fell but rose quickly, feeling no pain, and went on their way. Your usual day before Christmas.

This day was creeping across a little planet in a small solar system. The planet, called Earth, is a rocky oval filled with liquid lava; its surface is covered by thin layers of water, as well as by air, a volatile mixture of oxygen, hydrogen, nitrogen, and several other elements, each of which could pose a threat to its existence. Due to a confluence of favorable circumstances, life arose on this planet. This protein-based life, after millions of years, created intelligent beings called people, a group to which I, who write these lines, have the honor of belonging. Humanity, or the sum total of the intelligent inhabitants of the earth, has created civilization, which allows us to comprehend the universe (though not, of course, completely), aids us in combating the ancient misfortunes of human existence (and creates new and increasingly menacing ones), and permits man to take short walks in space while depriving him of the hope of great voyages into the depths of space. A most essential piece of information must be added here: life on Earth is subject to a strange rhythm which makes for quite unusual transformations of energy—birth and death, maturing and aging, being and non-being.

I am compelled to make these few superficial explanations in the hope that some copy of this book which I now labor over will reach the hands, antennae, or computers of other intelligent beings who may happen by our galaxy, intelligent beings from the central regions of the universe, from the more elegant neighborhoods of the Lord God's metropolis, beings better and wiser than we, the noble supermen of man's imagination. I write with such an ambitious, indeed unusual intention, only because I am bored by communication with my fellow men, my fellow wise men and idiots, my fellow prophets and scoundrels, my fellow torturers and victims.

Every year Christmas Eve brings us Earthlings a certain magical hope, awakens strange, exciting forebodings in us, and stirs our longing for our primal, unknown homeland. On that day, at the beginning of a winter or a summer two thousand years ago, a man was born whom we acknowledge as God, that is, as the co-creator of the unknowable edifice of the universe, a man who, in our belief, intercedes between us and an awe-inspiring, mysterious Supreme Being.

On this particular day before Christmas I was standing wrapped in a warm sheepskin coat in front of a jewelry store named, with no particular finesse, The Jeweler. There were about twenty people stamping their numbed feet behind me. I was shivering a bit myself, even though I was covered with abundant fur, shivering in anticipation of that day, of those few uncommon hours which might bring me, and all of us, some decisive solution.

"Look at that one, she's in good shape," muttered the individual behind me, a thick cloud of steam issuing against the collar of my coat. Eyes tearing from the cold, he pointed at the store's display window. "Just looking at that could get you in trouble."

The outlines of a woman's face could be seen through the dusty glass. A dark-haired girl with slightly indecent lips was looking out at the cheerless street with sepia eyes.

"Precisely, but not for us," I said melancholically.

"Why's that, we any worse than anybody else?"

Long gray hair protruded from beneath the fur cap of the man behind me, reaching down to the collar of his navy-blue jacket with orange piping.

"Maybe not," I sighed. "It's just that our birth certificates are slowly expiring."

"I, for one, feel young, sir."

"But you can't pass for young."

"You don't remember me, but I know you."

"You do look familiar."

"Don't bother yourself over it. I know you, that's all. When the time comes I'll tell you how."

I had already begun to regret having such a vexatious neighbor in line. But the man in the fur cap was smiling ambiguously. A flat leather bag, something between an officer's map case and a cosmetic satchel, hung from his hand.

"Would you like a smoke?"

"Thanks."

"Thanks, yes, or thanks, no?"

"Thanks, yes."

We lit up, no easy task. Glancing at the shop window, we saw the girl still staring straight ahead. Over at the intersection a swarm of people were pushing a stalled tram out of harm's way; it was moving along quite nicely, even clickety-clacking along the rails like a real train.

"I read everything you write," said the man behind me with a faintly unpleasant smile.

"Probably not worth it," I mumbled modestly.

"When the time comes, I'll tell you about it."

An old woman in a thin, frayed coat approached the head of the line. The cold was squeezing silvery tears onto her bluish cheeks.

"I'm an invalid," she began mournfully, but the line maintained a scornful silence. She wiped away her tears with a tattered glove. "My legs hurt me so much, so much I can barely walk."

She shifted from foot to foot, and indeed her legs did resemble two willow trunks. But still the line ignored her. Only one woman wearing a voluminous pelisse and an overlarge hat and fur-topped boots said ironically, "I'm not young anymore either, but still I'm standing in line."

The old woman wiped her tears.

"My husband died last year. I was left alone with the children. He didn't leave me enough to live on."

"Let her in," said a young man who looked like a student. A second youth, no doubt his colleague, tall, wearing a slovenly leather jacket, agreed approvingly. The line closed ranks, to defend its access to those elegant doors covered by lazy Warsaw rust. Whimpering, the old woman began gradually heading toward us. I occupied a strong strategic position beside the compassionate students.

"You've made your way in the world," muttered my neighbor, wrapped up in his own maniacal thoughts. "Who'd ever have expected it?"

"There's nothing to envy," I replied disagreeably.

"Duszek, meet Mr. Konwicki," he said, beckoning his neighbor with his hand.

I shook hands with a man in old-fashioned clothes with the elegance of the fifties about them. Duszek was over six feet tall and could easily have concealed a ten-pound weight in his hand.

"Now let me introduce myself. My name is Kojran." My hitherto nameless neighbor doffed his fur cap. "My name won't mean anything to you," he stated without any trace of disappointment.

"I do know you from somewhere."

"You're only saying that to be polite, Mr. K." Kojran smiled indulgently.

"It would be nice to have some liquid refreshment," interjected Duszek.

"We'll have to save our places in line. Look, Mr. K., she seems to have fallen asleep." Kojran indicated the display window with a move of his purplish ear.

The girl was still staring at the street, though traffic was now flowing normally and the trams were again moving slowly in packs toward Central Station.

"She's fallen into lethargy, I'm sure," said Duszek, coughing. Great puffs of steam flew from his mouth out over the heads of the people in line. "She's having pangs of conscience."

The wind was buffeting an enormous spruce tree decorated for Christmas which stood on the traffic circle at the intersection of several broad avenues. The tree was pulled every which way, as if bowing to the four corners of the earth, as if wishing to escape its confinement, its captivity in stone. Its red glass ornaments were showering down onto the trolley tracks like frozen sorb berries.

"My friend is French," said the student in a whisper, and the fat, red-haired youth in the open leather jacket nodded his head courteously.

"*Bonjour, monsieur.*" Kojran returned the greeting. "*Ça va?*"

"Yes, thank you," replied the Frenchman in heavily accented Polish.

"And what brings you here?"

"He's an anarchist," explained the student. "The police were on his heels, so he fled to Poland."

"Welcome to our beautiful country."

The Frenchman made a short speech in his native language.

"He says," interpreted the student, "that formerly every young European had to go to Paris. But nowadays one goes to Warsaw."

"That's a great honor for us," said Kojran, bowing again. The anarchist, too, bowed ceremoniously.

"It'd be nice to have a drink," sighed Duszek.

"We will when the time comes. How come you've got the shakes, Mr. K.?"

"See for yourself—red snow is falling."

"What do you mean, red snow? It's red from the neon. What are you waiting for, a miracle or something?"

There was a stone plaque on the wall of the building commemorating the spot where, during the war, fifty nameless people were shot; below it a paraffin memorial candle in a green jar kept flickering, then flaring back up again.

"Yes, you're right. I'm waiting for a miracle."

*

If our meager constellation were to be viewed from the depths of the universe, the denseness of the Milky Way would obscure our modest sun and our eight or nine (I don't feel like looking it up), our eight or nine planets—some with moons—those several small planets accompanying the sun, so important to us but a matter of such indifference in the jungle of space. One of those planets is our earth, where an incredible phenomenon occurred—life, life saturated with oxygen, that most infernal and deadly element. This earth of ours resembles a blue-green porcelain pear overlaid with a tattered white layer made up of capricious powdery puffs, the clouds revered by poets, the storm clouds which usher in cyclones and floods, and those terrible autumn low-pressure periods when people's hearts break, the ghosts of paralyzing premonitions creep from the mist, and life sinks into lethargy in its yearly attempt at eternal sleep.

On this pear-shaped planet, busy fulfilling Nature's commands, teem nearly five billion intelligent beings, or so these two-legged creatures with their erect stance would first appear to an eye or an electromagnetic wave. In the tangled process of evolution we divided ourselves into greater or smaller social groupings called nations, which perhaps makes it easier for us to vegetate. These great and small nations are constantly devouring each other in the struggle for existence, for endurance, for competition, according to the laws of evolution. Clearly it would be absurd to maintain that the small social formations absorb the larger ones, yet if one considers that those herds called nations suddenly swell and contract, distend and molder, multiply by gemmation, and become crippled by amputation, then, in the final analysis, they do devour each other (though sometimes it happens that one vomits out the undigested remains of a neighbor).

This strange division into nations is the source of much of our suffering, pain, and misfortune. The closer we come to the disintegration of nations as obsolete structures impeding the mysterious and terrifying process of evolution, the more intense the processes of ionization within nations becomes; the higher their internal and external temperatures become, the more tragic their collisions, those frictions we call wars, revolutions, or uprisings.

The tendency of writers, recording fictional or actual vicissitudes among particular individuals and among entire social formations, to tear themselves free of earth and to observe it from stratospheric heights or intergalactic space, is a mannerism which has now been examined by scientists and found to be a symptom of a particular aberration. But the description of life from the height of a fieldstone or a hydrant in a city is just as objectionable. On the whole, literature means abnormality, transcendence, aberration.

*

"Look, Mr. K., she's not there anymore."

"Who?" I asked automatically.

"Iwona."

The display window had clouded, obscuring the gloomy interior of the jewelry store.

"You know her?"

"Not yet," said Kojran.

"So how do you know her name?"

"It's Iwona," he repeated obstinately. "Shall we bet on it?"

"I don't like betting."

"You don't like taking a gamble?"

"Taking a gamble? Sometimes I do."

"But only all or nothing?"

"Exactly. Break the bank."

The thud of iron, the rattling of glass. Excitement rippled through the line. The poor old woman slipped adroitly in ahead of the students as the woman who managed the jewelry store opened its doors. The line edged its disciplined way into the store. Finally, we were standing beside a case filled with Soviet wristwatches and East German alarm clocks. Our ice-cold feet reposed luxuriously on a black marble floor. An enormous ceramic chandelier gleamed overhead (it should have blazed but there was a temporary power outage). From the back the manager brought out two candles stuck with scorched wax to an etui that had contained Chinese bracelets. Cheery little flames now flickered in the mirrors.

"Is that her?" whispered Kojran confidentially.

"Who?"

"Iwona. Over there, by the palm tree."

Our friend from the window was sitting beside a dusty little palm on an upholstered chair in the style of the False Duchy of Warsaw. She was reading a book with an air of peeved boredom. Her hair was almost black, there was something Creole about her complexion; she seemed Mediterranean, which somewhat dampened my interest. There is a certain easy beauty, a certain rashness of character and lack of restraint in those Southern peoples.

"Ladies and gentlemen," the manager's voice rang out. Her golden hair, combed back high on her head, trembled slightly. "Ladies and gentlemen, today's shipment has not yet arrived. It could come in an hour, it could come after the store has closed. I'm cautioning you now so there'll be no complaints later. The complaint book is temporarily at the bookbinder's."

A groan of disappointment, a violent surging of the line. Two men in cement-stained work clothes cursed loudly. A peasant woman with a large kerchief-covered bundle fastened to her front began to cry.

"Tough. We'll wait a little," bellowed Duszek over people's heads.

"Ach, these lines, these lines," sighed Kojran.

The woman in the voluminous pelisse and the overlarge hat turned to him and said emphatically, "They have lines in England, too."

I reached inside my warm sheepskin coat, my fingers groping for my jacket pocket. Nothing to worry about, the money was still there. Five thousand-zloty bills.

"Do you really believe in miracles, Mr. K.?" asked Kojran.

"Perhaps it's the first sign of old age, but I've started to."

"We'll settle accounts when the time comes. Miss Iwona, isn't that bad for your eyes?"

The Mediterranean girl lifted her head from her book and looked haughtily at Kojran, who sent her a kiss with two fingers, both of which had broken nails. Gradually we realized that it was not only dark but cold inside the store, which was why the salespeople were wearing sleeveless vests made of artificial fur. Sputtering in the gusty drafts, the little candle flames, like the leaves on an autumn birch, were trying to tear themselves from the black wicks.

"Boys," said Duszek, "we better find a couple of drinks or else we'll catch pneumonia."

"Wait a while. Let's get our place in line established first."

"Keep me in mind if you're going out for something," said a young man dressed completely in blue denim, bowing politely. He was twenty-sixth in line and now, with the addition of the poor dear old woman, twenty-seventh. He looked like some whimsical type from Le Drugstore in Paris or else straight from Broadway and Times Square.

Kojran and Duszek gave his proposal an ostentatiously chilly reception. Then, in a deep, hoarse voice, Duszek whispered, "Watch out, he's a stoolie."

A truck came to a halt not far from the store. A guard wearing a quilted jacket lowered the tailgate. The prisoners hopped down to the sidewalk. They were also wearing quilted jackets, except that they had orange vests over theirs. Each prisoner was armed with a snow shovel even though there was still very little snow. Maybe there'd be enough to shovel by the time the first star came out.

A sudden fear seized me. I had an idiotic desire to shatter the display case, along with the little boxes painted with scenes from Russian fairy tales and the Matryoshka dolls, one inside the other. But all I did was once again reach inside my coat, my breastbone in the clutch of a terrible and ominous pain. I massaged the ribs under my heart and slowed my breathing back to normal. But the pain did not go away, that pain which had been with me for several days.

Maybe it would be good to die right now, right here, with no time for any appeal, I said to myself. Ours is not an age for a leisurely, bourgeois death. Nowadays even shopkeepers, and, who knows, maybe even cabinet ministers, everyone prays for a sudden, unexpected end.

A little while later, my calm regained, I felt again, with vindictive satisfaction, my new acquaintance, pain, bite ruthlessly into my ribcage. My coat still smelled of the ram and the Alba dry cleaners.

"Oh, how I'd like to give them a good smack," snarled Kojran. "Twenty past eleven, no shipment yet, and there won't be any, either."

"In France they have to wait in line for hours, too," the woman in the pelisse said dryly. She even had overlarge emerald clips on her ears.

"You must be from the diplomatic corps," said Kojran.

"Why do you say that?" she asked, slightly offended.

"That's how they used to be."

"I'm just being objective."

"A Pole loses his temper when he has to wait," said Duszek.

"The Italians are more nervous."

"I don't care about Englishmen, Frenchmen, Italians," said Duszek irritably. "I care about Poles. Do you see what I mean?"

"I'm not going to discuss politics with you," she replied.

The peasant woman with the bundle took advantage of the moment of anxious silence to begin moving imperceptibly toward us. "Could any of you use some veal, maybe? I have some nice, fresh veal."

"Just don't stand here," said Kojran angrily.

"I'm not standing here, I'm only asking."

14

"Let's see the veal," interjected Duszek.

The peasant woman began untying her bundle. Grains of frozen corn spilled onto the marble floor.

"What do you need veal for?" asked Kojran.

"We can take a look and think it over. Veal's the best meat for you."

Just then the store manager leaned over the counter and said to the peasant woman, "Please step in the back with me."

The peasant woman froze in uncertainty, holding two legs of veal.

"But we were first," intervened Kojran.

"There's plenty, plenty for everybody," the peasant woman assured them, and slipped stealthily off to the back of the store, lured by the golden-haired manager. The girl with the book raised her head and looked at me as if she had seen me before, had been thinking about me, and wanted to say something to me. She suddenly shifted her gaze to the store window and the prisoners stamping their feet, waiting for the snow. Then she returned to her book.

Duszek blew a great puff of steam from his blue lips. "Guys, I'm begging you, it's high time to wet the Christmas fish."

"Right, the time's come," said Kojran impassively.

There was an icy wind blowing outside, a wind born out of differences in pressure in the earth's atmosphere. Sparse, smudgy clouds raced low over the rooftops. Those clouds concealed the brilliant light-blue sky, but we know that that pure sky is only a garbage dump into which solar winds drive packs of rusted satellites, half-eaten canned food, and human bones frozen for all time.

We started off toward a certain elegant restaurant. I was about to take hold of the handle on the glass door, which had a crack running its entire length, but Kojran stopped me without saying a word. We entered a dimly lit stairway, apparently the back way into the restaurant. With no surprise I recognized the smell of urine so typical of our hallways. We walked up a few stairs, our destination the second floor. Duszek rang the bell three times. There were traces of many business cards beneath the bell.

The door opened up halfway. The drone of a television set could be heard.

"We want to pay a holiday visit, pop," said Duszek.

A feeble old man supported by two canes let us into the apartment. While removing my coat, I checked again to make sure I hadn't lost my money. It was still there, rustling crisply in my warm pocket.

Suddenly the old man's legs went flying horribly out from under him. He saved himself from falling by a desperate manipulation of his canes and then, laboriously, led us into a small room. It was warm and cozy, the television flickering merrily with static. We sat down on a well-worn couch by a table covered with a country-style tablecloth. Photographs looked down from the walls, the faces touched up and larger than life. They could have been of the frail old man and his wife, no longer living, or perhaps they were of unknown people long dead, like the models of Michelangelo or Velázquez.

The old man returned, moving in his strange, jerky convulsions, and looked questioningly at us.

"How about some binoculars and jellyfish," proposed Duszek. "All around, naturally."

Something tinkled with a lovely, harplike sound. The corner of the room was damp from ceiling to floor. Large drops of dirty water streamed from the lamp, seeping down through familiar routes beneath the floor, on its way to the fancy restaurant.

"The guy upstairs's flooding," said Duszek, nodding knowingly. "He floods the whole house, top to bottom, about once a month. The plumbers have given up on it.

Today, my friends, every person should be self-sufficient. Each man should build his own house, plant his own potatoes and cabbages, and replace broken rain pipes or blown fixtures himself. We're heading in that direction. The age of specialization, my friends, is coming to an end. We're returning to a natural economy."

Our host swam into the room like a cuttlefish. Struggling with his canes and his condition, he was carrying a large serving tray. In front of each of us he placed two hundred grams of vodka in two tall glasses and a plateful of aspic of pig's feet. And this was binoculars and jellyfish.

"Mr. K., to our fortunate meeting."

We each drank down a hundred grams. I drank nervously, in two gulps; Kojran poured a careful unbroken stream directly into his throat; Duszek took short sips as if drinking spring water. I had bolted the alcohol down and with spiteful indifference was now feeling what was transpiring inside that bucket of bones doctors call the thorax. Beneath my necktie that lead vise was still clamped to my breastbone.

"And so, you don't remember me at all?" asked Kojran.

"You know, I used to remember every face I had seen as a child, every name I'd read, even if it was in the newspapers. Now somehow everything's gotten all mixed up. All faces seem familiar and completely unfamiliar and the same's true for names. It's chaos, but without the dynamism of chaos."

"But it's a shame you don't remember me. That'd be something to talk about."

"A few years ago I was traveling through America. I spent two weeks in New York. The entire time someone kept leaving his card for me at the front desk requesting I call him. The signature seemed to bring back some old memory, but it could just as easily have meant nothing. I preferred the latter. Finally, I was buttonholed in front of the hotel by a terribly emaciated, sickly old man with heartbreaking eyes. I knew who he was immediately, even though I'd never met him before. He took me to a cheap restaurant around Sixtieth Street. We ordered hamburgers, which were served by a Negro with hair like an African cannibal and a button on his shirtfront with an aggressive slogan: BLACK IS BEAUTIFUL. So, while biting into that suspect hamburger, I felt myself choking up with a kind of fear, shame, sudden pangs of conscience. The old man, barely able to breathe, was seven, maybe ten years older than I, almost my contemporary, and he was at death's door. He looked at me with lifeless eyes but eyes burning with a final brilliance. And though this may sound stupid, I assumed a military posture (even though I was sitting) and a military, official tone and reported to him as to the subsequent fate of our partisan division from early 1945 on, our fate which had separated from his, for he had been arrested in fall 1944 and had escaped from a prison transport. He escaped across the ice of some forgotten lake under fierce fire from the escort, then, under tragic circumstances, made his way to the West, where his endless wanderings quickly took their toll on his health. Now he was dying, dying, and yet unable to die at home on Long Island; he'd been dying for an endless time, constantly thinking of his distant Poland, constantly meditating on those six years of war, those best six years of his life when he was handsome, powerful, noble, when he had influenced the world, when he had been establishing a better, wiser moral code, when he had been a man with the form and likeness of God. So I made my vastly outdated report, picking at my hamburger and salad with Russian dressing, while around us, on all Manhattan's streets and avenues, a great world crisis was wreaking havoc: hippies chilled by the first light frost were singing of love, the

Arabs were waging war with the Israelis, Palestine commandos were shooting women and children and hijacking planes, homosexuals were marrying, philosophers proclaimed the cult of chaos and the absurd, young filmmakers were making films which lasted several hours and showed some nameless man sleeping, addicts were smoking marijuana, women were stripping naked in bars day and night, Europe was attempting to unite with the United States, an African president was preparing to be crowned emperor, in China the government was organizing a revolution against itself, a few men were orbiting earth in a primitive capsule resembling an iron barrel, old men were masturbating in porno theaters, a junta of colonels suddenly resigned, the Church was debating the abolition of celibacy, somewhere someone was soaking himself in gasoline and burning before the eyes of the world, elsewhere an earthquake, a flood drowning a city and its people, a poet weeping over a poem disfigured by the censor or by a printer's error, while I was submitting to an outlandish convention, one which either died or was murdered thirty-odd years before. So, submitting to a defunct convention remembered only by myself and perhaps also by the man sitting across from me, I related the odyssey of a small detachment of young people who had wanted to change the world and soar above their provincial cosmodrome of sparse marshes and wild forests, a crater of misfortunes and anonymous crimes of little concern to anyone. And so this was my meeting with my commander, whom I had never met before, and who himself had never set eyes on me, the commander of my war, which no one remembers anymore, which is now so little remembered that it might as well never have happened."

Kojran lifted his second hundred grams of vodka, held the glass to the light, and stared at his portion of translucent narcotic made from mild Mazovian potatoes.

"Did you know I'm going there, too, Mr. K.?"

"Where?"

"America, of course. I'm flying there tomorrow morning. On the first day of the holidays. If a miracle doesn't happen first. Let's drink, for we do have something to drink to, isn't that so, Mr. K.?"

"I have my doubts on that score. My head's started spinning a little and I'm starting to slur my words."

"What are you saying? I know you. It used to take a half pint just to calm you down."

"That time has passed. I have a trip ahead of me, too."

"A long one?"

"Yes. To Kalisz."

"Not so far, then."

"For me it is."

A gray-haired man with an accordion slung over his shoulder entered the room. Without looking at us, he picked up a music stand and carried it off to the next room.

"Drink makes a Pole merry," pronounced Duszek, raising his glass.

"But aren't you curious why I'm going to America?"

"Must be either for the UN or to see family."

"You guessed it, Mr. K. I'm going to see my brother."

He drew his leather bag from under the table, undid the gleaming clasp, and began rummaging through his documents. "I've got everything. Passport, visas, even dollars, all I have to do is get on the plane and fly to America, but I don't know if I will or not."

"If you'll fly tomorrow?"

"If I'll fly tomorrow, on the first day of the holidays. My brother has a gas station with a house of worship on the second floor. Of the gas station! Two floors, that's all there is. The second floor's fantastically big and it's a

Catholic church, a synagogue, a Protestant church, maybe even a mosque. They all take turns praying there. One day one religion, the next day another. And right under them my brother with his gas station and little repair shop. Doesn't that surprise you?"

"A little, but not all that much."

"Why don't you take this little pill?"

"I'd drop on the spot."

"No, you wouldn't. Let's go back to the jewelry store and do our shopping."

> In the silent night a voice rings out:
> Arise, O shepherds, to you a God is born . . .

We froze, empty glasses in our hands. In the next room the street band had begun warming up. Our host, his legs flailing to the four corners of the world, appeared in the doorway.

"The musicians won't bother you?" he asked.

"Let them play, why not," said Kojran.

Through the rectangle of the door I could see the backs of the musicians, all dressed in identical light-blue coats. The guitar player was leading the familiar refrains of Christmas carols in an apoplectic voice.

"Can I bring you something else?" asked our host.

"We've had enough," answered Duszek. "We came from work. We're standing in line."

The old man nodded knowingly, and then with a sudden spasm left the room.

> The shepherds come to Bethlehem,
> And trill their lyres for the Infant Christ . . .

"They're singing off-key, goddamnit." Duszek scowled and then said to the aspic, "Don't tremble and I won't eat you."

"You've got problems, too?" Kojran said, leaning closer to me.

"A few. Well, maybe two."

"That's not so much."

"For me it is."

"I'll tell you something. I used to write poetry."

"Who didn't?"

"Ah, it's hard to talk with you. I used to be completely different. Along the way, in the last twenty years, they've cut everything out of me. Everything they could—half my stomach, my appendix, tonsils, varicose veins, lung lobes, the meniscus. Enough?"

"Sure, that's enough for anyone."

"I think I've lost a lot. I've changed, Mr. K."

"And on me things have started growing. Over the last twenty years."

"Like what?"

"Cysts, varicose veins, a hump, myoma, corns. I've changed, Mr. Kojran."

"You never heard my name before?"

"I think I might have."

"Look through your papers. I think your mother might have been born in Kojrany."

"So, are you from Kojrany?"

"No, I was born in Mickuny."

"Kojrany, Mickuny, Niemenczyn, I'm from those parts. That's my native country. But I don't think I was ever there."

"I heard you were, that you were from there."

"Or else I talked people into believing it. Genealogy by erudition. I've read so many reminiscences, memoirs, monographs that, extracting their essence, I could have fashioned a modest literary genealogy for a homeless man, meaning me."

"Now what are you running on about, Mr. K.? You

have a normal biography. I know. I was supposed to shoot you in 1951. I followed you for three weeks with a pistol brought in from Wilno."

> *God is born, the whole world trembles,*
> *The Lord of Heaven naked born . . .*

The street band was attempting a third carol. Each of the musicians had already had their binoculars and jellyfish. Water was trickling silently in the corner, trickling without disturbing us, soaking down into the luxurious restaurant, which had no customers.

"I bring up something interesting and you don't say a word," said Kojran softly.

"I had the feeling death was on my trail. In '51, '52, maybe even '54."

"No, not later on. In '52 I was already in jail with Duszek guarding me. Isn't that so, Duszek?"

The giant gazed melancholically at his enormous hands.

"Why bring it up. Maybe the whole thing's a big lie."

*

I wonder how I write. I have never read a book of mine in my entire life. That is, I read them all while writing them, I read over the individual sentences I've just written and struggled with. I read while I write and write while reading, but never have I reached for a bound volume still covered with its original dust jacket and seen the letters become my words, from the start of the first chapter to the final period, one short infinity away. But I am not really curious, for if I were, then I would have read those withered pages on the sly from decades back, or a few months back. I hate my prose. I hate it like a ghost, a bad memory, like pangs of conscience. That prose is like some sort of discharge oozing from my organism. As if it indicated that something were scarring over, that something were healing, but in fact nothing has scarred over, nothing has healed.

We are divided into large, medium, small, and totally microscopic communities, each speaking its own language. These closed societies are distinguished from each other by differences in articulation, by how sounds are issued from the larynx. There is such a multitude of these sonorous and cacophonous sounds that we are unable to make ourselves understood to each other without the aid of persons known as interpreters who have learned several or even a dozen or so languages—different ways to issue sounds by means of their voice box.

But it is even more difficult for us to communicate in the sphere of experience and the consciousness that comes from experience. We understand individual words, entire sentences, quite extensive paragraphs, but we cannot necessarily understand the person who wrote them.

I am an individual who is not understood by his fellow men on the Tiber, the Seine, or the Hudson. They may understand faithfully translated major or minor sentences of mine, they may grasp the meaning of a metaphor, flickering moods, but they will not be able to empathize with my fate or embrace the meaninglessness in my meaning, which will seem to them unrealistic, alien, lacking motivation, and thus completely incomprehensible. They do not understand me because I am a Pole, because I belong to a community spread out along the Vistula River or rather to a community swarming around a great European river. But the fate of that pack of intelligent beings roaming nomadically beside a wild river, though falling under the biological norms and laws of earth, is a tangled fate, a complicated fate, a fate which causes degeneration, like every misfortune, every calamity. For that reason my daily life, my usual waking thoughts, my despair at night, the chemistry of my brain, and the physical structure of my soul are beyond the understanding of a member of a close-knit, stable, sleepy society suffering from sluggish digestion. And for that reason he will say that I am incomprehensible, that I write incomprehensibly, that the situations I evoke, the forebodings I rouse, the fears I hold at bay are unconvincing, lacking in expression, alien. Shifting the responsibility onto me, he finds me guilty of being incomprehensible and I feel ashamed. I explain myself, I beg forgiveness, until the moment finally comes when my patience is exhausted and I say, You should thank God that you don't understand me and pray every day that you won't understand me for as long as possible, for, in the end, you will have to understand me and understand me fully, with the last vibrating fiber of your nervous system, with the most sensitive, quivering membrane of your mind, and that will happen when you come to share my fate, when, like a hail cloud, my *fatum* blows over to the West and stands above your country, your home, your head, when the torturers of the Great Destiny drag you from your warm bed and begin endlessly torturing you with a hopeless daily life, gags, shackles, begin slowly chipping away at your brain, persistently poisoning your heart, and in the final moments of your unhappy existence you will see the indifferent, uncomprehending, senseless eyes of your fellow men who live by the Vistula, the Vltava, and the Potomac. Incomprehension can be a sign of lofty nobility, the nonchalance of a higher mind, the absentmindedness of a spoiled child, but incomprehension can also just as easily be the first stage of lethargy, the first eclipse of the agony, the first signal from providence that years of terrible plague are emerging from the rim of non-being.

But there are other reasons why I am incomprehensible. I write in code. I use prison slang more often now, I have mastered the complex arcana found in the notes smuggled in and out of jails. My writing is the blackened walls of a cell, a cell on death row. On those walls, marks to note the passing days have been scratched, maxims of hope heady as a summer's day, warnings to free descendants, and brutal cries of despair when it becomes impossible to live and impossible just to die.

I no longer strive to be understood. I no longer depend on your approval, your sympathy. Now I write only because I must. I do not believe anyone will read what I write and understand it as fully as I did while struggling with the resistant, constricted, ephemeral words. I write because some strange sense of duty impels me to this paper, which in ten years will turn to dust. I write because in my subconscious there stirs a spark of hope that somewhere there is something, that something endures somewhere, that, in my last instant, Great Meaning will take notice of me and save me from a universe without meaning.

*

"Did you fall asleep?" Kojran nudged me with his elbow.

"I was thinking about my life."

"You weren't thinking about anything."

"A Pole gets sleepy when he thinks," stated Duszek.

On the television, the face of the announcer flashed amid the swirling static; he was saying something and had been speaking non-stop and without conviction for fifteen minutes. Drops of water the size of cherries were dripping from the black, mud-filled lamp.

> The shepherds came to Bethlehem,
> Played to the Infant on their lyres . . .

The band had achieved a certain fluidity and was playing freely, purely, like a philharmonic orchestra. With bloodshot eyes, the musicians stared out through the dusty window at the snowstorm flying through the city like an express train.

"I'll go home for Christmas Eve drunk as a lord," I sighed in despair.

"Who knows how this Christmas Eve will end?"

"Are you trying to frighten me?"

Kojran poured the last drops of vodka down his throat. "But it's you who's waiting for the miracle."

"That's true. I'm keenly aware of that miracle now, the strange exciting aroma of that miracle, I can hear the heavenly voice of that miracle, really not so much a voice as a mysterious murmuring, an astral clinking, the restless sound of pulsars, white dwarfs, black holes. Some knowledge is creeping toward me from that infinite junk pile, some sort of simple formula for meaning, the peace of understanding is trickling down to me."

"I owe you a bullet. A slug in the back of the head."

"I know. I betrayed the old faith for the new one. Then the new one for the old. But I never wanted to betray anything or anybody. Treason and loyalty, vice and virtue, love and hate, they still haven't solved anything."

> *Let us all go to the stable,*
> *To Jesus and the Virgin . . .*

The accordion player was playing for us. Standing in the doorway, his dark fingers dancing on the keyboard, he was staring at us with a fixed, somehow slightly unctuous gaze.

"Mr. K., those were the remains of our organization, the very one that brought you up. They passed the sentence. I was to carry it out. Do you know I'm three years younger than you, Mr. K.? Back then three years was a lifetime. Your death was to have been a warning to shock and remind those who were vacillating, those who were exchanging the old Poland for the new one."

The snowstorm was sealing up the windows. You could no longer see out. We were dozing in a great, warm snowdrift. An old man three long years younger than I was blinking his eyes to wipe away his blurred tears.

"Yes," I said, lulled by the carol. "I remember at the beginning of '45 I, too, was involved in carrying out an order to kill a traitor. I would have, too, but circumstances intervened. But perhaps we were carrying out the order collectively. I used to be able to remember it clearly, I think my conscience even bothered me about it. Later on it all got erased, though, and now I can't remember a thing. As if I were remembering my own sins or someone else's or mankind's sin in general."

"I followed you for three weeks. Weren't you having a little affair at the time?"

"What? I was never much for affairs."

"You're being secretive. Why deny it? No, it's not secretiveness, it's hypocrisy."

"In our parts everyone was a little on the hypocritical side. Including you."

"Me?" Kojran sighed, rolling a balled-up piece of bread along the table. "I didn't have any time for hypocrisy. Duszek taught me about sincerity, isn't that so, Duszek?"

"When evening comes, a Pole starts reminiscing."

"Evening's a long way off. I followed you everywhere. To your editor's office, to the Legion swimming pool, to bars, meetings, grocery stores, dates, though you may deny it. I was following you all the time with my pistol and your sentence written out on a piece of notebook paper. I had ten thousand chances to shoot you but, for some reason, I didn't do it. I kept waiting for something, and to this day I don't know what it was. Then they grabbed me and I did six years. Because I, too, was being followed closely by what was left of the organization, my organization and yours. You might say we were walking Indian file."

I looked at his common face, his poorly shaved throat, the slightly greasy collar of his polo sweater, the kind only provincial activists wear now.

"But, Kojran, you're lying. You just felt like upsetting your neighbor in the line. Isn't this just a waste of energy?"

"My energy is free, it doesn't cost anything. So when you were leaving Wilno for good, where did you hide your arms?"

"I don't remember. It's been so many years."

"You remember all right. It was in the Rudnicka woods, on Insurrection Hill. True or not?"

"Kojran, I was trading in salt bacon the whole war."

"Ugh, what a faker you are. That pistol came from that grave you dug. Maybe you used to carry it yourself? Right, Duszek?"

The giant wearing a suit from the fifties, a suit which could be back in fashion any day, this unfathomable giant spat with dry lips at the television set.

"Leave me alone. I quit and that's that."

> *He lies in the manger, who'll run*
> *To sing carols to the little one?*

Our host squeezed his way into the room like a crab. He was carrying an oil lamp, though night was still a good way off. The window was a wall of cottony snow. A white mound had covered the Paris of the north.

"What's the lamp for, pop?" asked Kojran.

"For light, the electricity's off."

"What are you talking about, the television's working."

Our host froze on his canes like a frozen bird.

29

"It really is working, the goddamn thing, even though there's no electricity. That's an ornery machine for you."

Outraged, he called in the musicians. The band of disabled veterans watched the flickering image of a man and a woman learning Russian; they rapped the screen, looked inside the set through the slits in the back, then helplessly returned to their music stands. Our host was also not bothered by this obvious freak of technology.

"It'll go off when the time comes," said Kojran, displeased with all the commotion. "You see, if I'd have killed you then, you wouldn't be here now."

"If you'd killed me then, I wouldn't be here now," I repeated with a sense of wonder. "An entire mountain of things would never have happened—stretches of boredom, anxiety, unbearable sorrow, mistakes, some shame, some low-level exaltation, vain hopes, and the constant pain of trying to understand, fathom, penetrate, and know some peace. You know, I'm so close to it that I can touch it with my nose, but I still can't see it yet."

"Are you looking for pity?"

"No, just running off at the mouth."

My right leg had fallen asleep under the table. I started bending and straightening it, bringing it back to life. I could feel a little tingling in my toes, as if I were walking on moss or on the wild herb called savory.

"You're a terrific smartass. I've been observing you for years. You're like this." He made a snakelike movement of his right hand, which was speckled with liver spots. He had been taken early. I, too, would be taken early.

"Yes, I am a bit on the sly side. But I never profited by it. All my slyness goes right up to the sky like smoke. Doesn't bring anybody any light, any warmth, any energy."

"Ah, what you need is a punch in the mouth."

"Kojran, you have no manners. Why should we drive each other crazy here. I'm leaving, see you."

"Sit down and listen. Duszek, tell him how you met me."

"I don't feel like it. One binocular and you start insulting people."

"I've lost my resistance. And who was it that knocked it out of me?"

"Spare me the allusions."

"But I'm your penance, after all. Your rosary. A rosary with as many beads as I've got vertebrae."

Someone started hammering his fist against the front door. The band broke off, only the balalaika continued to play for a crestfallen moment. Our host was grappling with someone in the doorway. Outside, the arctic, a blank, impenetrable whiteness.

The man dressed all in denim entered, trying to brush off the old cripple.

"I've been looking for you everywhere, and look what I find here, glasses, a bit of home, and some good Polish talk." The new arrival smiled politely.

"Watch it, he's a stoolie," Duszek warned hoarsely.

Kojran raised his glass, but it was empty. He had drained it to the last drop.

"You wanted to tell us something?"

"The goods have arrived."

"Real nice of you to remember your elders. And you, Duszek, you're always mistrustful. Let's get going, gentlemen."

I reached into my pants pocket, where my little nest egg was tucked away, but Kojran raised his hand to stop me. "Easy does it. I'm paying."

"It's my turn to show some gratitude."

"You will when the time comes."

He settled the bill with the old man, then slapped him on the back so hard it made his metal crutches clang. The band was getting ready to leave, too. The accordion player closed his accordion with an asthmatic whine.

"I won't say, 'Till tomorrow,'" said Kojran, "because I won't be here tomorrow. Good luck in your business."

"God bless you," said our host. "Long as they're here, I won't go under," he said, indicating the floor which concealed the first-class restaurant.

*
* *

Suddenly you stopped in your precipitous, feverish flight and hung like a skylark above that green crater filled with the chaotic rubble of the city. Chortovgorod, Devil Town, as Tsar Nicholas I had called it when he served there as a youth in a regiment of the guards.

It was the most singular of times, as the poets might say. Behind you the sun was already rubbing its red belly on the edge of the horizon, an enormous, swollen sun, a sun from the end of the world, a sun which third-rate artists would use, a hundred years later, in their movies. You hung above the green, curly crater which held in its tight embrace more than a dozen churches, the same number of stone palaces, a few hundred crooked, tumbledown, abandoned wooden dwellings that smelled of moss and looked like sleeping birds. From this city, this Rome of the north, a gray-blue cloud had arisen, a mist and miasma of hardship and misfortune. The sounds of church bells drifted in that mist, that air of death, and, among them, treading heavily, was the somnolent, sinister sound of a Russian Orthodox church bell.

You looked at that city stunned by a fever of longing, fear, and ominous foreboding. You looked at it then as I would now, at this hour, at the end of the road, at the edge of the endless marshes.

But you were warmed by your youth, spurred on by hope, by your turbulent faith, which you had retained in the dismal cells of Petersburg's School for Military Engineers, at Mieroslawsky's courses on warfare in Genoa, and when wandering cold and hungry through the Balkans.

Then you ran down the wooded slope cooled by the first clinging layer of night. You entered a labyrinth of little streets where the spring mud had yet to dry. Groping your way through the thick twilight redolent of May bugs, you sought your home with its glowing eyesocket of a kitchen window.

Stealthily, like a spy, you walked into the large entry hall, listening to the convulsive rhythm of your pulse, smelling the air dusty with mildew, the dead aroma of baked bread, the waning ether of shriveling fruit. You stood in front of the door to your home, a pale gleam of light from the house fell onto your chest, your overcoat.

Then suddenly the door opened and in the faint swaying light of an oil lamp you saw Rozalka freeze in midstride.

"Jesus, Mary! Be gone, vanish, you nightmare!" she cried hysterically, slamming the door.

A little later you heard your mother's heavy, uneven footsteps and her whispering as she walked: "Don't be afraid of the dead. They come to ask us to pray for them. Come look, you'll see there's nobody out there in the hall."

The old door groaned open. Your mother stood in the doorway covering the glimmering light of the oil lamp with the palm of her hand. Her gray eyes looked upon you without fear.

"Is that you, Zygmuś?" she asked, crossing herself and then making the sign of the cross over your ghost.

"It's me, Mama."

"Every ghost praises the Lord God."

"It's me, Mama. I've come back to you for good."

And you embraced her, warm as she had been in your childhood and in your memory. Then she began weeping softly.

"Mama, why are you wearing mourning?"

"Because you died, my son. You are no longer among the living."

The baby in Albertyna's arms started to cry. She began rocking it monotonously back and forth. Rozalka stood by the stove, her eyes gaping wildly. Suddenly you felt like laughing, laughing merrily and lightheartedly as you had long ago in your now forgotten childhood.

"Mama, I've come back. I've come back for the uprising," you said in a whisper.

Then, with slow caution, they drew near you, their cold fingers touching your face, hair, and the rough cloth of your overcoat. The baby in Albertyna's arms began to speak, gurgling through its tears. I, too, returned as you did then, and I still do on autumn nights or in the fever of my ever-more-frequent winter illnesses.

I, too, remember that kitchen with its huge white-washed stove that could bake ten loaves of bread at a time or food enough to feed a hungry crowd. I remember that old sideboard which divided the kitchen in half, and I remember that makeshift bed beside the sideboard on which you, and perhaps I, too, on which we both dreamed of an uncommon life, a dazzling fate, an exceptional destiny.

Later on you sat down at the table and they, poor, unfree people, gathered up all the treats that are saved for those special occasions which, as a rule, never happen.

"Mother, sisters, I have seen eternal snows, endless summer; I have walked thousands of kilometers and lived through thousands of bad days; I have known friendship as well as hatred; I know all that is good and evil in this life. Mama, we are about to launch a great uprising."

"Shhh, quiet, child," whispered your mother, closing the window more tightly; a silent, patient spy could be standing outside.

You sprawled there at the table like an old soldier telling stories of the great world, the great universe of Europe, which was now raising its fist against Moscow.

"Zygma, did you hear the bells ringing at dusk?" asked Albertyna. "They were ringing them for you, at the Church of Our Lord's Angel, brother."

"But I'm still alive, sister. I've come from the land of Italy, back to Polish land."

Just then a carriage flew down the street by St. Catherine's Church. You heard the fierce yelp of harness bells, which fell silent among the houses but not for very long.

"Shhh, quiet, child," your mother whispered again, and only then did you really see her greenish-white hair and the far-off look in her eyes.

Rozalka held up an old scrap of newspaper to the light. "Zygma, look, your name's printed there. It says you perished at Grochow in General Langiewicz's detachment. They said a sacred Mass for your soul in all the churches today. The whole town is praying that you be granted eternal rest."

"Those Muscovites would like to bury us all."

"Shhh, quiet, there's somebody out in the hall."

"Tomorrow, the day after, all Lithuania will rise."

Then from somewhere down below on the banks of the Viliya came the sounds of trumpets and drums. The frightening alien clamor of a military tattoo woke the drowsing town and put it on its guard.

One of your friends slipped in with news of the cause, a neighbor woman dropped by to borrow a little something, and thus grew the conspiratorial ring of your admirers who, on that fitful autumn night, marveled at their twenty-three-year-old hero, the messenger of freedom.

Then came the time for parting, a separation for a short stretch of mortal danger, or perhaps forever. Everyone wept, including you. Your mother made the sign of the cross over you with an old crucifix from her native Balwaniszki. You, of course, thought to yourself that this was how Byron had set out for death and glory, but you did not know that many other generations of twenty-year-olds would, in just the same fashion, bid farewell to their family homes and that I, too, one December night, with the exact same message, would walk those snow-covered country roads, eighty years after you, that I, too, would set out to fulfill your ambiguous and still-unfinished fate.

So, you walked from your house and no one saw you off for fear of spies. You turned around once, and then once again, to bid farewell to that old, misshapen house, a house, of course, similar to mine, an orphan's house, a house no longer yours but one that you would always remember as your nest.

The streets were empty; only once in a great while would someone (obviously authorized to move about by night) appear in passing, lantern in hand. In a fog thick as smoke, fifty Cossacks flashed by, their leather scabbards slapping the bony flanks of their horses. Around a corner, out of sight, their commander whistled shrilly, his fingers in his mouth, and the fifty Cossacks raced off at a full gallop. Within seconds, the dark heads of women appeared in a few windows. The town had been feigning sleep, waiting tensely for a sign, the first sign of freedom.

Then you turned into Subocz Street, low, poor, always knee-deep in mud. You passed the Baroque apparition of the Church of the Missionary and suddenly the small street became a country road watched over by old trees petrified in anxious expectation.

The road forked by a roadside cross and you went the

way I always used to, taking the road to the left, which led down to the bank of the Viliya. Then a large moon rose, with the shadowed features of a good-natured face, or perhaps those of the shores of continents and oceans, the moon, threshold to heaven. Back then the moon shone brightly, shone the way the moon is supposed to shine, for in those times boundaries had not yet eroded, summer was different from winter, one sex was different from the other, life was different from death.

In the small, ancient village of Markucie, dogs barked at you, a warm wave of air bore the aroma of night-scented stock, somewhere a poorly fastened well handle creaked; you caught sight of a railway embankment which still looked raw, covered only with scanty hairlike grass. The sound of a great rumbling carried from Puszkarnia, as if some supernatural creature were being born there; the thudding rumble grew, and then, in a lake of steam, belching sparks and fire, the great hulk of the train swam past like an ominous ship. It was the Petersburg train bearing hateful people and ill tidings.

"Poland is not yet dead!" you cried out suddenly to the depths of the empty valley which was later to be my happy world. That cry merged with the thudding of the train's cast-iron wheels as it rolled on toward the city, the unforgettable Chortovgorod.

You ran through steep meadows toward the river which flowed toward a broad hill whose oaks were old enough to remember the Lithuanian dynasty of the Giedyminits. It was bright, the way it is on a cloudy, misty autumn day and you seemed to see old witches bent beneath their sacks, out searching for secret herbs in the dewy grass.

Beyond the small wooden bridge joining the sandy shores of the Vilenka was the Tupaciszki farm hunched on the slope of a hill. You had barely stepped into the shadow of the enormous poplars when you heard the dry sound of the watchman's rattle.

"I see you! I see you!" cried someone in a senile voice. "Who has God sent us here?"

"I'm here to see the squire. Mr. Jozef Sulistrowski," you answered mechanically.

An old man carrying a soot-blackened lantern and an oak stick appeared. He took a careful look at your Polish overcoat, your boots of Russian leather, and then, with no further questions, led you to the farmhouse, which was not much larger than a peasant's hut. The whitewashed walls were phosphorescent in the cadaverous moonlight, the windows covered by wooden shutters with small black embrasures reminiscent of old frontier forts.

The watchman walked up to the back of the farmhouse, rapped his stick on the corner, and quickly called out something in a plaintive voice. Finally, a meager reddish light fell through the slits in the shutters, followed by the hospitable clang of iron bolts as a tall man carrying a candle came out onto the porch. He had wrapped an overcoat around him against the damp night cold.

"Who's here? Who's looking for me?"

"I am Zygmunt Mineyko. I have a message for you, your honor."

"Oh, it's you. We've been waiting a long time. Please come in."

In the old drawing room with its sagging ceiling, by the flickering light of the candle, you saw the furniture wrapped in coarse slipcovers. A few French newspapers lay casually on the large table.

"I need a knife," you said. "And then I will report to you."

"Wandzia, bring him a knife!" shouted the tall, valiant man with the blond hair.

"Which knife, Jozef?" asked a high, melodic female voice.

"Doesn't matter, my love, as long as it's sharp."

A girl wearing a cap covering her head came into the room. You knew that she belonged to that race of swarthy, dark-haired frontier girls found nowhere else on earth.

"Wandzia, let me introduce Mr. Mineyko, an officer from the military school in Genoa."

You bowed, adding, "And a member of General Langiewicz's detachment."

You cut open a thick seam in your overcoat and carefully withdrew a scroll of thin paper. She crossed her dark arms over her breasts, examining you with eyes that shimmered with the colors of moss and heather; they had that sort of eyes, those girls in whose veins flowed the blood of the Lechites and Lithuanians, Karamites and Tartars.

Sulistrowski brought the candle closer and read the paper carefully, finally thrusting one corner of it into the flame. The letter of introduction curled into a charred scroll.

"Let me embrace you, Zygmunt," he said, as he approached you and hugged you like a brother. "Are you hungry, do you want to rest?"

"No, thank you. I'd like to assume my duties at once."

"I like that. Wandzia, don't stand there doing nothing. Bring out food and ambrosia."

She ran silently from the drawing room while Jozef continued hugging you with his bearlike paws. "Good, excellent, now we'll smoke those Muscovites out. Lithuania is a mound of dry tinder; a few sparks and it'll burst into flame."

Wandzia returned with a large blue bottle and meat wrapped in a towel. She prepared the snack, peeking curiously over at you. You could not keep your eyes off her, and for the first time in your life some absurd sorrow gripped you by the heart, as they used to say back then.

Sulistrowski must have noticed something, for he made a jolly threat to you: "I recommend caution to you, Zygmunt. This is my new young wife, and that meat there's still left from our wedding."

At that moment you heard the sound of distant rifle fire. The candle flame flickered from an unseen puff of air. Stung by sudden fear, you cocked an ear as Sulistrowski said softly, while moving toward the door, "It's war. That's right. It's already started. I'll draw up appointment papers for you immediately. Wandzia, entertain Zygmunt, but in a fashion befitting a young married woman."

The watchman was shaking his rattle outside the window again. He was singing matins or perhaps talking to the dogs, who had woken up. The candles cast shadows on the soot-blackened walls.

"Are you married, too?" asked Wanda, without raising her eyes. "It's hard to live alone."

"I never had time. I never stayed in any one place long enough. A soldier's life. Maybe after the war, when the country is free."

"What will the country be like then? People say different things. Maybe you know?"

"It will be different. Just, noble, intelligent. An example for all of Europe. An uprising begun with the blood of our finest sons."

"May God grant it," whispered Wanda, and with a sudden rush of panic, you noticed that her lovely breasts swung freely beneath the thin cloth of her blouse when she set the glasses down and filled them with a trickle of nuptial ambrosia.

"God will grant it because God is with us," you mumbled so as not to startle the young woman. You thought you could smell her, a smell of sleep, lovage herb, and impetuous love.

Sulistrowski appeared in the doorway. "Zygmunt, what name do you want for the uprising? Have you given it any thought?"

"I have. Let me be Maciej Borowy. Since my family traces its descent from the forest."

Sulistrowski vanished into the side room, Wanda kept bustling around the table, although everything was already quite nicely laid out. That Wanda reminded me of Jaskółka, our liaison officer, who was arrested in 1944 and vanished without a trace, vanished without a trace before having known physical love or the pain of motherhood, the joy of freedom, the humiliation of slavery.

Sulistrowski returned, stood in the center of the drawing room, and, handing you a piece of parchment, solemnly announced: "Colonel Borowy, here is your appointment as military leader of the Oszmiana district, by fiat of the Division of the Lithuanian People's Government."

Once again he embraced you and kissed you on the mouth.

"I will not betray your trust. Either freedom or death."

"Freedom or death," repeated Sulistrowski. "Wandzia, tell Konstanty to harness up the wagon, the one in the barn."

"Do you want to travel by night?" she asked, sleepily removing her cap, which had tilted askew on her pitch-black hair.

"It's best at night," you replied gallantly. "I'm late as it is. They're ready to drive out the Muscovites without me."

She shook her head and her hair spilled down onto her shoulders. She went out quietly into the hallway. It was then that you heard the whining hum of a mosquito straying at the boundary of light and shadow.

"Well, Colonel, let us drink to the success of our cause in arms."

Then it was time to part. You stood in the hallway, Sulistrowski already dressed for the road, Wanda shivering from the night cold.

"May God keep you in his care," she whispered.

You caught the brief aroma of mint and felt the astonishing warmth of her lips. For a moment she snuggled up against you as if making a ritual gesture. You suddenly felt a great heat, heat and some sort of unfamiliar regret. That was the second time that night that strange new sense of regret had come over you.

"That was the first time I ever kissed a woman," you whispered, without knowing why.

She moved lazily away from you. "You'll find one for yourself after the war."

"If I come back."

"You will. I know it. I had a good dream just before the watchman started rattling."

"So, until we meet again, Wanda."

"May it be soon, my young Colonel."

The worthy britzka which had been kept in the barn was comfortable as a carriage and bounced merrily along the potholes of the unpaved Oszmiana country road. The moon was almost at its zenith, illuminating the aquamarine fields and the now motionless, silent woods. The horses moved at a walking pace; at times they'd spring briefly into a trot when you came to the top of a sandy hill. Konstanty would wake them up with the reins if they began dozing off in the narrow ravines of a backwoods. It was a night for lunatics and for ancient ghosts to come creeping out from the bogs.

"Jozef," you heard and woke suddenly.

Sulistrowski came to with a start and reached under the seat, where no doubt he had something concealed.

"What is it, what? Do you see a patrol, Konstanty?"

"I don't see any patrol, but I can tell you, this is tough on the horses."

"Ah, Konstanty, you're always feeling sorry for the horses. Who are you saving them for?"

"Not for nobody," rasped the coachman insolently. "I feel sorry for the horses. People act stupid and the beasts have to suffer."

"Jozef," you repeated. "This strange night and gulping down this air of ours, some sort of force is entering me. There will be a Poland, Jozef."

"At first, you'll get four hundred volunteers. They'll arrive in a day or two at a prearranged point. In a week you'll have double that. All our young people are hiding in the farms, settlements, forests, all waiting for a sign."

"God be praised, Jozef. When I look back and see how many miles had to be covered, how much cold, hunger, and sickness had to be endured, how much help had to be begged from people, I know it was all worth it for a moment like this."

"Use the reins, Konstanty. What happened with General Langiewicz? People say all sorts of things, but no one can get at the truth. Can you tell me, in all confidence, Zygmunt?"

For a long while you said nothing.

"After winning two battles at Chrobrz and Grochow he crossed the Austrian border and surrendered. I'll never know why."

"Does it always have to be like that for us? The soldier fights and sheds his blood, and the commander gives away the victory."

"This time we'll have young commanders, leaders from another school. And once we feel weapons in our hands, there's nobody who'll take them away from us."

"May God help us," whispered Sulistrowski.

43

You thrust your hand into your shirt and felt for the piece of paper which made you dictator of your native district. The moon had set unnoticed and the night was pitch-black. The horses slowed their pace. They moved with their heads lowered to the ruts in the road, snorting every now and again. But at that very moment, the horizon, invisible till then, began to brighten.

"Ah, Poland, Poland, dreamt of, prayed for, and suffered into being," you sighed. "I can almost see you emerging from the mist, the gloom of night, the cemetery of nations."

Dogs began barking near the horizon, which had now brightened and turned green. Konstanty halted the horses.

"There's Oszmiana. Should we go past it or right through?"

"Go right through town. It'll be quicker."

The britzka rolled past the chimneyless cottages at the outskirts of town. As if sensing danger, the horses stopped snorting and stepped lightly between the ruts along the sandy rise.

"Know where you are?" whispered Sulistrowski.

"Not at all. Everything looks the same at night."

Accompanied by the barking of dogs roused from sleep, you rolled past the black, hostile-looking houses. Then, with a sudden sense of relief, the horses broke into a trot. The sand flying from the wheel rims began singing more eagerly.

"The Russians are deep sleepers," said the coachman, now more cheerful, his tone containing both admiration and a dash of mockery.

"Let them sleep. They have a long way home ahead of them," you answered with a sudden rush of joy.

"Head toward Wolozhin, Konstanty, and don't spare the horses. There's a courier waiting in the pitch factory there. We'll find out what our colonel's situation is."

Then it was woods again, a great forest which widened out to the south joining the Bialowieza forest on the other side of the Niemen River. You felt you were riding into an age-old kingdom and you were its ruler, severe and just.

"Hungry yet, Zygmunt?" asked Sulistrowski.

"No. I have no appetite at all. I just want to get to my soldiers as fast as possible."

"That's all right. We'll have something to eat at the pitch factory. The horses can use a little rest."

Dawn broke. A few red drops fell from the hood of the carriage. Birds began singing in a thicket. The last of the night's clouds had sailed past the horizon for a day's rest.

"Are you going to make a revolution as Garibaldi taught you?" said Sulistrowski.

"I'm a soldier. First we have to liberate the country," you answered cautiously.

Sulistrowski shot a glance at you from the corner of his eye but said nothing.

Then, by daylight, you turned off the wide road and burrowed into an old, gloomy forest thronged with ferns tall as a man, where even the birds were silent. The only sound was the warm wind wheezing through the dark tops of the trees. The britzka's iron rang and jangled as it bounced over the log-sized roots of ancient spruce trees. At last a small and now probably forgotten clearing came into view. You saw a hut without chimney or windows and a soot-blackened stove for burning coal.

"Whoa." Konstanty brought the britzka to a halt, jumped down from the coach box, and began thrusting his hand under the harness to check whether the horses had been chafed, muttering to himself in a language of his own.

Then from behind the hut came an old peasant wearing a dirty shirt that hung down to his knees and carrying a rake as if he were on his way back from haying. He bowed low, removing his sheepskin hat.

"God be praised, is the squire going to Balwaniszki for the festival?"

"Here is your leader for the uprising—Colonel Maciej Borowy."

The old peasant looked you over closely, blinking his faded eyes, finally showing his bluish gums and his single black tooth. Then he fell suddenly to his knees, trying to pick you up by your legs.

"My dear, dear boy, we were praying and praying for you. So you're alive, then, you poor boy?"

You took him under the arms and lifted his light body up in the air and kissed his cheeks, which smelled of tobacco.

"I see you know the courier, Zygmunt," said Sulistrowski in surprise.

"Of course, I used to carry the colonel in my arms," said the old peasant proudly. "I used to be steward for the colonel's father, may he rest in peace."

"That's a good sign, that's more than a good sign," said Sulistrowski, taking out the basket of food.

You sat down on a black tree stump. Old Jan tore the stringy roast carefully apart, his gaze fixed on the wall of the forest. Sparrows who still remembered the presence of people in that wilderness appeared out of nowhere.

"Shall we drink to a swift victory?" asked Sulistrowski, offering traveling cups. The old peasant carefully set his aside on a resinous tree stump.

"Jan, why aren't you saying anything?" prompted Sulistrowski. "Drink to a swift victory and tell us when our troops will come."

The old peasant was chewing hard on a tough mouthful. "Right now there's no troops," he said, still looking at the forest.

"What do you mean, no troops?" Sulistrowski leaped to his feet. "And where are the four hundred volunteers promised us right from the beginning?"

"They were here, but they all went back. They had to make hay, the rapeseed is ripe. A lot of work in the fields right now, sir. So they left."

"That can't be!" shouted Sulistrowski, close to apoplexy. "Who dared dismiss them?"

"They were raring to go when they got here. Oh, a lot of them came too, sir. Brought weapons, too. And there's no words to tell you how they went after those Cossacks. But they waited and waited and no leader came, so they all went back home."

"Nobody stayed, nobody waited to see how the situation would develop?" you asked, your throat tightening.

The old peasant raised his eyes to you, looked at you a moment, and his expression seemed to soften.

"One detachment stayed. They waited. They'll come to the meeting place tomorrow."

"Many men?" you asked, aware of the sound of your heart.

"I didn't count. There'll be around twenty, thirty young men."

"You hear what he's saying, Jozef?"

Sulistrowski was already hastily packing his basket.

"Time is short, Jan. You better go. Everyone should bear arms and present themselves on King's Hill tomorrow at dawn. You know where that is, Jan, near the crossroads, just before Rosoliszki."

"I know, I know," muttered the old peasant, looking for his rake. He took a moment to think and then, raising his sheepskin hat, said, "Seems to me everybody'll get going once they hear a graduate of the Genoa School's their leader. They'll come to the uprising, why shouldn't they come," he said, trying to convince himself. "They'll be there at dawn."

At that moment you thought that the old man was comforting you and Sulistrowski without believing it himself.

"Konstanty, hitch up the horses!" shouted Jozef. "Dogs, scoundrels, sons-of-bitches. A straw fire, a Polish straw fire. They felt like going home. They'd had enough fighting. Teach them a good lesson, Colonel, teach them a good Genoa lesson, so they dream of Garibaldi in their sleep."

"He'll ride the horses to death," grumbled Konstanty. "Then there won't be no horses and none of that Poland of theirs neither."

Jan had vanished. You looked all around the clearing but it was quiet and peaceful everywhere, not a blade of grass was trembling; the sparrows, too, had fallen silent after stealing the last of the crumbs.

"Jozef, can this be?" you asked, your lips dry.

"Let's get going, time is short. You know what our people are like. One minute they come together, the other they go back home. Now they'll come back again. Maybe not four hundred straight off, maybe three hundred, maybe two hundred at the worst, but you'll have your detachment, you'll raise the entire glorious district of Oszmiana from its knees and strike at the Muscovites. Konstanty, you're wasting time."

You jumped into the britzka, which had grown colder. Sulistrowski lowered the hood impatiently as if he were closing the visor on a helmet, and clucked up the horses, since Konstanty was looking apathetically around the coach box for his whip.

"It began just like this," you said softly.

"What are you talking about, Colonel?"

"I was remembering Grochow. The sad consequences of a victory not taken advantage of."

"It's shameful to hang your head. I can tell you haven't seen much failure in your short life."

"Oh, Jozef, there's been a lot, too much, even. But I kept pressing on toward Lithuania, pushing on for so many months it was like climbing a bare pine pole. I dedicated everything to it, everything a young man can."

"You did well, Colonel. Your country won't forget you."

Konstanty looked around and said, as if to the sand ground by the wagon wheels, "Every government's the same. It's all the same to a simple man."

"But you're a Pole, after all, Konstanty. Don't you feel your Polish soul in you?"

The coachman cut a branching roadside fern with his whip. "I'm from these parts here," he said, and then quickly crossed himself.

At noon you reached the meeting place, a crossroads where by a strange coincidence three old poplars stood with their pitted trunks grown into one. Konstanty immediately hung feed bags on the horses' muzzles. You jumped down onto the thick, juicy moss scarring the seldom-traveled road. A cuckoo began to sing in the damp shade of the pine forest. In spite of yourself, you counted its unhurried, pensive notes.

"I almost forgot," sighed Sulistrowski, returning to the britzka. He groped under the seat and removed a bundle wrapped in sackcloth. He undid it carefully and, holding it in both hands like a tray of food and drink, he handed you a new, gleaming black revolver. "This is from me. May it serve you well."

You thrust the weapon in behind the tail of your coat. Slippery and cold, it clung to your shirt. Sulistrowski rubbed his hands, smiling uncertainly. "Chin up, Colonel. Tomorrow you'll have a detachment and be a commander."

"God willing."

"I'm not saying that everything's working out perfectly. But, Zygmunt, there will be a Poland." He hugged you harder than necessary, as if consumed by vague pangs of conscience.

Then he quickly mounted the britzka, and with sudden eagerness Konstanty lashed the tired horses. The carriage wheeled around, its dry separating wood creaking, and it began rolling back toward Oszmiana, toward Chortovgorod, toward that old life that you had left forever behind you. Sulistrowski looked back only once; you stood, hands by your sides, beneath the three-trunked tree that whispered pagan prayers.

And before you, just as it would be before me half a century later, lay the future—unknown, mysterious, majestic. Your unknowable fate, the country's Golgotha. A hot, sultry hope; an inspiring, ardent premonition. You were twenty-three years old. You were five years older than I, and eighty years younger.

You walked into the wedge-shaped area formed by the crossroads and lay down on a sandy hill in a whortleberry thicket. You looked up at the sky through the black boughs of spruce trees, a sky that was yours, a Lithuanian sky, but one that still looked much like the alien sky of St. Petersburg and the foreign sky of Italy.

I want to remember what I was thinking at an equivalent moment. I want to reproduce that mood, that sense of things, those dreams from the wondrous time of youth, perhaps not so much wondrous as biological, pulsating, breezy, light, not burdened with the weight of experience, not poisoned by disappointment, not drugged by discouragement, youth which passed like a tumultuous spring storm.

What were we thinking about on that invisible threshold of time? Ourselves? Poland? I don't remember anymore and I don't know how to summon it up from the past now dead or rather fixed forever, those moments of inconceivable self-enchantment and humility, audacity and fear, greedy hope and foolhardy uncertainty. In just the same way I do not know how to summon back that Poland which we bore within ourselves like the overwhelming pain of the first spasm of a coronary. That incorporeal Poland, Poland, that hypnotic phantom.

You were surrounded by a day of wilderness, a day which seemed to stand still but which passed very slowly, almost imperceptibly, moving without the slightest rustle through the ancient trees toward the west, trailing behind it the damp burden of night. But the day was still full of condensed, resin-saturated light. You heard the forest move lazily between pauses of terrifying, bottomless silence. Somewhere a woodpecker was rapping at a tree, a horsefly buzzed; caught in a tangle of flowers, a badger crept past, a fallow deer galloped by, its head held haughtily high, a tree broken by a spring hurricane cracked and fell, a light wind which had strayed into those ancient spaces stirred impatiently.

You chewed on bread baked from rye ground in a hand mill. You sucked on the sweet chunks of grain, thinking of the young woman from the previous night. You recalled each individual gesture, each bend of her head, each elusive smile, each movement of her breasts inside her cambric blouse. And from those minute instants of a woman's beauty you wished forth an image of a woman's body, a naked body, a body still unknown to your eyes, and to mine, to your hands, and to mine.

You sensed something stirring within you. Something pulsing, uneasy, swollen with heat. You were straddled by a sinful desire, which exuded the sultry stench of herbs and decayed flowers. Transfixed by the eyes of red clouds, you felt a fierce love, perhaps for the last time, for a woman you did not know, a girl you had not met, a lover who did not exist.

Then came the night. The night of a young commanding officer before a great and unknown battle. Clasping the handle of your pistol, you paced back and forth among the quiet trees. Above you millions of stars were on the move. Your familiar Milky Way sent you greetings and it seemed the universe was gazing at you with God's unseeing eyes.

Finally, just before dawn, the rumble of a distant wagon reached your ear, followed by a sound like that of people treading carefully. You took the safety off your pistol and crawled over to the three-trunked poplar, which had fallen silent, bent over some mystery of its own.

A moment later the heads of horses came into view, their eyes shining phosphorescently.

"Stop. Who goes there?"

"Friend," came the reply. "The white eagle has arisen."

"The Lithuanian coat of arms and the Archangel forever." You uttered the countersign hoarsely.

A tall man with a double-barreled shotgun slung over his shoulder walked up to you. "My name is Mokrys. I've brought you twenty-eight volunteers."

"And the others?"

"The others will arrive in a day or two."

"The others will arrive later," you repeated.

One of the volunteers, who knew the forest, led you to a nearby clearing, a large meadow cleft by a dark stream. You set up camp in the shade of enormous oaks which stood guard at the boundary of the tall wild grass. The first of the volunteers had already tossed off his clothes and jumped into the dark current; the water's deep voice resounded, the cheerful yells of the young men echoing off the bluish wall of the still forest.

"Colonel," said Mokrys, "here's a bag with the proper amount of money for you to pay out at the appropriate time. And here is a trusty sword which will stand you in good stead."

You kissed the sword's hilt, worn smooth in the hands of generations of soldiers. You strapped the sword to the belt of your insurrectionist's coat.

"I shall not fail to join your detachment, Colonel," added Mokrys. "Look for me in a week or two among the divisions."

"So you're leaving, then?"

"Organizational matters detain me for the moment. But not for long. I'll show up to do my duty."

A flock of cranes landed in the bogs on the other side of the stream.

"I have my own detachment," you said to yourself.

"Yes, now you have your own troops. Now, in God's name, you can get started," said Mokrys softly.

And like Sulistrowski he embraced you in brotherly fashion, kissed both your cheeks, while you thought with sudden fear that there probably had already been too many such ceremonies, that the ritual of declaring war was being drawn out too long.

"Time for me to go," said Mokrys, again looking up at the empty sky. "Be well, Colonel Borowy, may we meet again soon."

He jumped up on his four-wheeled carriage covered in chapped leather, then moved swiftly off between the hazel bushes where the road began, a dirt road which led into the heart of the forest country. Without thinking what you were doing, you shook the new money bag, which someone had embroidered beautifully, and heard the clinking of the rubles, which had been collected by unknown people, for Poland, for the resurrection of the country.

Then you called an assembly. Your troops formed in motley dress, armed as if for a hunt. There were no scythemen among them, no peasants armed with scythes able to cut and pierce in hand-to-hand combat.

"I was promised peasants with scythes," you said in reproach.

No reply came from the two uneven lines of soldiers. So you walked in front of them, inspecting your division. One face seemed familiar to you.

"What's your name, soldier?"

The dark-faced young man hesitated for a moment and then whispered almost confidentially, "Chaim Karnowski."

"You're an Israelite?"

"No, a Pole of the Jewish faith."

He had no weapon. A sturdy oak stick banded with formidable steel was clenched in his hands.

"I recognized you too, Colonel," he added, after a moment.

"How do you know me?"

"We used to fight by the temple when you were still in high school, Colonel."

"Work hard and I'll make you a non-com."

Later you began teaching drill to those twenty-eight raw recruits. You ran them ragged for four hours, until you were finally able to pick out the quick-witted, those gifted for the craft of war, whom you would make the officers of future companies and battalions.

You established sentries around the camp, which was filled with the songs of nightingales. That year even the nightingales sensed the uneasiness in the air, and their trilling was heard not only during the short nights but during the days as well, in the drowsy heat of noon. The rest of the young soldiers had efficiently built a field stove and had already baked some tasty bread made from the flour that was part of their supplies.

The smell of fresh bread, the age-old aroma of domestic tranquillity, wafted over the meadow; intrigued, wild birds lifted their heads over the marshes, covered their lustrous eyes with the film of their eyelids, and looked as if they were delighting in the warm, burning smell of the still-damp campfire.

You found yourself a comfortable spot by an oak tree and began sketching out plans for fastening bayonets to the barrels of aristocrats' shotguns. If there was to be a shortage of scythes, a substitute cutting weapon, able to withstand a Russian attack, had to be devised. At that moment you felt like the twenty-three-year-old father of that group of your peers, just as I had felt myself the father of fifty-year-old Belorussian peasants. And I, too, experienced those emotions of a leader, those raptures of domination, those joys of an action already underway.

The sun was already moving toward the western wall of the forest. The most able men, those who would become officers, spontaneously resumed drilling the recruits. With overwhelming amazement you heard commands in Polish while the forest stood in silence, as if observing the birth of something forgotten, damned, forever forbidden.

Then a patrol approached, leading an old man wearing a linen shirt and linen pants who was carrying a half-empty, dirty sack and a gnarled stick. The old man was ageless. His faded, shaggy hair, which fell closely onto his forehead, his yellowed mustache, and his never-shaven beard, all this hair could have equally well concealed a man of thirty or an old man around fifty. His faded eyes looked with impassive calm at the guard energetically prodding him.

"We caught a spy, Colonel," reported a stripling in an old Hungarian fur coat.

"He was circling around our camp."

"He was peeking through the bushes," accused the others.

The old man rubbed one bare and dirty foot against the calf of his other leg, keeping a stubborn silence.

"Did you search him?"

"Yes, Colonel. But there's nothing in his sack except for some old bread. Not even a scapular."

You looked him over. He looked back at you with a distant curiosity not of this world.

"Who are you?" you finally asked.

"A man."

"And what's your name?"

"What do I need a name for? Do I own an estate, do I rule over men, do I display ambition? What do I, a simple man, need a name for? God has even begrudged me a nickname."

"What were you looking for?"

"I wanted a drink of water from the stream. The water here's like medicine. You should see how it changes color in the sun. It's a healing potion, that water."

"You've got an agile tongue."

The beggar shrugged his shoulders. It was the first time his immobility had been broken by a gesture, but this was not the gesture of a beggar—it had a touch of the drawing room.

"I meet all kinds of people on the road and it's God's will that I exchange a few words with each of them."

The raw youth in the Hungarian fur coat moved forward angrily. "He's making up stories, Colonel. The Muscovites have set spies everywhere. There're more spies than people now. An oak branch for this one, and that'll be that."

The beggar raised his lifeless eyes to you. "And who gave you the right to kill people?"

"We are insurgents," you answered.

"The Leviathan has spread his wings and savage claws and covered the whole world. You, leader, have come from afar and you will return to distant lands where the sun never sets. Your earthly affairs are dust, ashes, vanity."

"You collect alms?"

"That I must. I have all my life and I will till I die."

"And what if I have you tried? Are you aware that the entire country is rising against Moscow?"

"States rise and fall. Man is made in the likeness of God. Man is a free bird."

The soldiers stared at you, tense with impatience, awaiting your verdict. The beggar pulled out a crust of burnt bread and began chewing it casually. He looked up at the sun, which was already dissolving into redness at the western edge of the sky.

"We have not found any proof of your being a spy. But since you might betray us without meaning to, I am ordering that you remain in our camp until the moment we leave. Understand?"

"I can stay, why not? I'll do some singing. Winter's far and death's not near."

He tied up his bag and set off toward the stream. Not far from the stove he sat down and began rocking back and forth, probably saying his prayers.

"He's an Old Believer, Colonel," said the young man in the fur coat in a quiet voice.

"Possessed is more like it," doubted the captain of the guard, who was armed with an English carbine.

"Whoever he is, he goes his own way. But so as not to tempt fate, keep an eye on him."

Night fell. The beggar sang or lamented until dawn. No one tried to stop him. Day returned. The soldiers drilled, but with less enthusiasm now. The beggar sang again the next night, a strange song, as if he were presaging some evil, portending misfortune. Some soldiers nudged him with the butts of their shotguns or flicked their whips across his back. But nothing did any good. The beggar continued yelping ceaselessly on the same spot by the stream, near the stove in which bread was no longer baked, for the flour had run out.

Karnowski approached you and stood respectfully beside the cleft trunk of the oak tree. The soldiers were dozing in the bushes. No one felt like drilling anymore.

"He's bad luck," whispered Karnowski, averting his head.

"I can't let him go. Whatever is fated will be."

"Whatever is fated will be," agreed Karnowski.

For a while you remained silent, observing the brightly colored butterflies fluttering near some blooming flowers.

"What would you do in my place, Karnowski?" you asked suddenly.

"No one would have appointed me to your place."

"I've staked my whole life on this one card. But it is not possible to go to war with some twenty raw recruits."

"Maybe the reinforcements will still arrive, Colonel."

"And maybe they won't, if they haven't so far."

"I have no place to go back to. I ran away from the cheder."

"I have no place to go back to, either. And I don't want to go back."

"Better to die."

"One must die in battle. You know what I think, Karnowski. I'll disband the division, we'll wait on the farms until a party is organized, a real party like the one that was promised, with at least four hundred men—armed, trained men. Then we'll rouse Oszmiana province and the whole country as far as the Niemen."

Karnowski did not reply, he was driving dried acorns into the ground with the end of his stick. The young recruits rose from the grass to watch white flotillas of wild swans flying north across the sky.

"There's no other course. Tomorrow I'll order them to disperse."

Karnowski knocked the peat off his stick and started walking toward the nameless stream where no one felt like swimming anymore. A cold night breathed out from the motionless walls of the forest. The floodwaters of the stream flared red from the glow in the west. A bird whined monotonously on the other side of the stream. But a choir of nightingales prevailed. Their strong pure voices sang out from several sides, but I know that this was no accompaniment to love but proprietary cries. In their song, you, however, heard that romantic music which brings a sense of unfulfillment to mind and awakens regret for a life that shall be no more.

The hungry rebels were chewing hare sorrel, spitting out gobs of green spit. You walked over to them; you wanted to talk, to dispel the bad mood, but somehow words failed you and you did not say anything. The beggar was lying on his back, his hands behind his head, looking at the water, which held the brick-red of the sunset and the deep black of the oncoming night.

"I'm letting you go tomorrow," you said softly. "You'll be free tomorrow."

"I am free. Free as a beast in the forest."

"Yours is a senseless freedom. We will give the people real freedom and we will give it to you as well."

"An individual can be free; a collective, a herd, a mob, never. Freedom is a gift from God."

"Where do you come from?"

"Nowhere."

"Who were your parents?"

"I've forgotten. I'm from these parts. From these forests, these crossroads, these backwaters."

"I must have met you before in my life. I remember your voice and your eyes."

"You probably met somebody like me. There's always been people like me wandering the earth, and their pilgrimage will last till the end of the world."

"And aren't you ashamed?"

"Ashamed before whom?"

"Before us. Look at those young people who might not be alive tomorrow."

"What do you want?" he snapped. "Go to the devil."

And once again he was the foolish, haunted beggar. He began singing his prayers or yelping to the anemic sickle moon.

The young man in the Hungarian fur coat had found a glowworm. He held it in his closed hands, watching its aquamarine light through the spaces between his fingers.

"What's your name?" you asked.

He sprang obediently to his feet. The glowworm fell into the dewy grass.

"Ildefons, Colonel. Ildek, for short."

"Ildek, go check the watch. So no one falls asleep on me."

The boy in the fur coat found his glowworm. A little green flame in his hands, he set off cautiously into the boundless spring night.

You returned to your quarters beneath the old oaks. You did not know then that someday King's Hill would be called Insurrection Hill and would be so designated on the ordnance maps issued to high-school-age partisans during the greatest world war. The calls of the nightingales were growing louder and louder, and it even could have seemed that from somewhere very far away the warm smell of night-scented stock, the smell of a tranquil Polish home, had come wafting in, borne by the cold.

Suddenly you were seized by a strange fear, a fear you had never known before. The fear of defeat, misfortune, failure. The fear of a conspiracy of evil powers. Fear of fate's mockery. Fear of your own weakness. You wanted to jump up from the damp ground and flee wherever your legs took you. To run, take the shortcut through the ancient forest. But to where? To what? To whom?

Just at that moment you heard a crackling in the brush. Someone was approaching from the depths of the night. Many tired-looking men.

"They're here, Colonel. Our men are here," gasped Ildek emotionally.

A dozen or so of your rebels sprang up from beside the fire which had been made the night before beside the dead field stove; they held up resin-smeared chips of burning wood to illuminate the new arrivals, who were led by a short, stocky man wearing a Russian army coat stripped of its epaulets. He lifted his hunter's cap in greeting, revealing a large, bald, sweat-lathered head.

"Major Nawalkiewicz, at your service," he said in a hoarse voice. "Who's in charge here?"

You rose slowly from the ground, where a wisp of river mist was creeping into the depths of the forest.

"I am Colonel Borowy. Please show me your documents."

Instead of documents the leader of the newcomers pulled a felt-covered canteen from his shirtfront. He took a gulp, wiped off the spout, and said, "Take a belt of this juice, friend. Nothing like it in the whole province."

"We don't drink here, Major. But I would like to see your papers."

His detachment responded with uncertain laughter.

"We've brought you our heads, my boy, that counts for more than papers. We've been dodging about like a bunch of rabbits through fields and forests for three days to find you."

"I expect you took the necessary precautions."

"I did. I never let the Cossacks get closer than a verst to us, isn't that true, boys?"

"That means you were observed by the Muscovites?"

He drew closer to you, surrounded by a stinking cloud of homebrew. Bringing his thick lips to your ear, he whispered hoarsely, "There's more gallows than people in the city. Muravyov has built another city of gallows. They're hanging Poles at every corner like boars. And you're asking me about papers. Nobody gave me any papers, friend. There were supposed to be forty men and in the end barely ten showed up. People are scared terrible. Muravyov the hangman swore to the Tsar he'd hang all the Poles. So that's how things stand with us."

You felt like the huge oak trees were crashing down on your head one after the other. The resin chips spitting red sparks went out with a melodious sizzle. The major's men stood in silence, as did yours. Everyone was waiting for a word from the colonel. And you, the young leader who had roamed thousands of miles back to your homeland, surmounted terrible discouragement, great weakness, and a dreadful spiritual crisis in yourself, said, "So, the Muscovites are already aware of our presence. In that case, we must withdraw. Tomorrow we will pull back into the heart of the forest. It's not worth waiting anymore. It's time for battle. Well, thank you, Major."

The major was about to embrace and kiss you, but he

stumbled on a root and grabbed hold of the rope belt on your open coat.

"You can count on me. I know the business of war. I fought the Chechens for three years in the Caucasus. I almost had Shamyl himself in my hands. The Grand Duke himself pinned the cross of St. George on me. You know, I've taken a liking to you, son."

"They were fighting for their freedom," you said, horrified.

"Who?"

"The Chechens. They were rising up against slavery. Like us."

"So does that make me a villain?" asked the major, flustered.

"But maybe now the Chechens are with the Russians on our trail."

"So does that mean I did right putting my bayonet through them?"

"Major, kindly order your men to bivouac."

"You wouldn't happen to have a bit of the old sauce about, would you, son?"

"We don't drink here."

"You know how to fall asleep on an empty stomach?"

The new men moved off toward the fire, where they mixed with yours. A buzz of lively conversation arose. With increasing frequency you heard the sinister name Muravyov uttered with pious fear. Large bats were zigzagging silently over the clearing.

Major Nawalkiewicz suddenly emerged from the darkness again. He was shaky on his feet, his red eyes darted furtively about, and he sighed heavily.

"Have no fear, Colonel. I may talk like a Russky but I'm a Pole. I'm from these parts. The Muscovites took me as a soldier that year; you can't remember, but maybe you heard about the year '48. I was something then, you can ask people, ha! Well, then came twelve years in the service, hard service. I fought Chechens and Turks and Circassians. But now you say fighting Chechens wasn't good? Still, maybe you can find me a little drop? The thoughts that fly about my head at night! So what do you think, will there be a Poland, eh?"

You said nothing. He shifted from foot to foot, blew his nose, elegantly holding it with two fingers, then slouched off toward the fire, which was showering streams of giddy sparks into the black night.

You dozed until dawn, your dream and waking states intermingling. You saw real Cossack patrols, real artillery crews, and the almost tangible silhouettes of enemy soldiers leveling their bayonets at you. And you dreamed of the fire, the sleepy soldiers wavering in the blood-red light of the fire, and you dreamed of a clearing full of river mist.

When the sun rose attended by dark clouds, you and your soldiers, with a sense of renewed hope, recited a prayer together, and then you ordered them to march. River water was poured on the last of the fire, the unneeded wagons were dispatched, and a marching column was formed on the high road. The youth with the English carbine unstrapped the detachment standard, the standard of your party; you appointed him standard-bearer. Ildek in his fur coat with his cousin or neighbor immediately came forward to assist. On that fur coat, too warm for those spring days, too wide for those narrow shoulders, on that provincial, out-of-style fur coat, you could still see the remnants of the basting, the final traces of a mother's careful hands. After all, I too set out one December night in a home-sewn coat like that, a great bear of a coat, a mourning coat, a wisp of tow from the nest of home.

A brisk wind caught the standard and sent the

amaranthine field with the Polish Eagle and the arms of Lithuania in white unfurling above the soldiers' heads. You set off to the south, leaving the beggar you'd freed in the middle of the road. The bearded wanderer watched you for a long time, then raised his hand and made the sign of the cross.

At the sound of the tramping of all those feet behind you, a sudden joy descended on you from the clouding sky and you struck up a song which had been sung by the cadets at the officers' school in Genoa:

> *O roses, our roses!*
> *O how terribly long*
> *Will the blizzard yet roar!*
> *Let's plant roses for the summer to come!*

More and more of their strong voices joined in. They liked the song right away and perhaps some of them had sung it furtively at home on endless, rainy spring nights.

> *Driven from our native fields*
> *We may never see those flowers,*
> *So let us plant them then for others,*
> *Plant them for a better world!*

An enormous flock of jackdaws wheeled overhead in the darkening sky. A few drops of rain fluttered in the maple leaves.

> *How beautiful and sublime our fate!*
> *Where we go the hawthorn blooms*
> *And we leave roses when we go.*
> *So let us not depart this path!*

After several hours' march, the advance guard reported to you that there was a small forest village up ahead and no possibility of bypassing its dozen or so huts.

You brought the detachment to a halt at the side of the high road. The weaker ones lay down at once on the dry leaves left from the previous year. Those who were more resourceful were already ferreting about in the grass in search of sorrel.

You took the bag from Mokrys and divided the money among the soldiers.

"You can buy food in the village," you said. "The major will be responsible for order, I'll give the signal to regroup on a hunting horn."

"So you're going to take us to Warsaw on foot, then, is that it?" asked Nawalkiewicz acidly. He wiped the sweat lathering his forehead with the back of his hand. It was obvious he had no taste for a forced march of that sort.

"The Muscovites are afraid of the forest. The deeper we go into the wild, the more dangerous we are."

"They'll follow us to hell. I know them. I keep smelling their stink in the air."

They set off for the village, a disorderly bunch. You remained at the edge of the forest. Feverish chills ran down your back and you knew it was the onset of an attack of that fever you'd brought back from Turkey. Once again drops of rain, heavy as hail, began falling. The sky had been walled off by drifts of black cloud, but the jackdaws had appeared again above the motionless treetops. They chatted monotonously with each other, describing large circles above the woodland clearing cleft by the uneven scar of the high road.

A wagon of the kind favored by Jews came galloping out from the village. The major himself was driving it, his hat lost in some burst of energy. Your excited soldiers and an even more excited Jewish merchant were running after the little one-horse wagon.

The major stopped short beside you and jumped

down from the wagon. "I brought you medicine. Give me money," he said triumphantly. A small cask bound by brass hoops lay on the wagon.

"Major, this is no time for carousing. We're on the march."

The major walked over and looked you in the eye knowingly. "I know all about southern fevers, friend. I was in the Caucasus, Balkans too. I watched you sleeping, son. I had the shakes myself last night. A little raisin wine never hurt anybody and for us two it'll be a real help."

The Jewish merchant approached you now, bowing almost to the ground. "I request payment, your honor, your excellency. My horse is for business, not for galloping. Your rebels took everything in my store. They ruined my entire business."

You tossed him the bag with the rest of the money. He caught it in flight and, without checking its contents, thrust it eagerly inside his shirt.

"Keep your tongue behind your teeth. Tell no one you saw us."

"That goes without saying. May God grant you wise and healthy children, your honor."

He quickly jumped onto the empty wagon, lashed the horse's belly from beneath with his crop, and then sped away toward Oszmiana, galloping even faster than the major had. Meanwhile, the rebels had tapped the cask and the clear wine was already flowing into cups and canteens.

"Karnowski! Karnowski, over here!" you called.

He ran up to you military-style, holding his head-basher of a stick. His thick, curly head of hair was already wet from the first drops of rain. Black, curly hair covered his intense black eyes.

"What do you think—will that storekeeper betray us?"

"There's no guarantee. He's an ignorant man. He could

betray us from fear or stupidity." A touch of sadness could be heard in Karnowski's guttural voice. He resented that you chose him to question about the storekeeper.

"It doesn't matter anymore. They know anyway." A fit of trembling shook you, a fine rain had started again.

"Let it pour—it'll erase our trail."

"Wait a minute, Karnowski. It won't be long before things get turned around—we'll do the pursuing and they'll run."

"I'm of the same opinion, Colonel."

"So, go to the rear guard now and keep a careful watch on the high road."

By then the cask was empty. One bruiser lifted it over his head and hurled it into the dense buckthorn bushes. Major Nawalkiewicz handed you a Russian canteen bubbling with a quart of raisin wine.

You drew a few sips of the sweetish liquid into your parched throat and choked with sudden nausea.

"Went down wrong," observed the major. "You're used to Italian or French wines, friend, but around here you have to make do with Jewish wine. Be smart, drink for your health's sake, because that fever's got you shaking like dung."

The whispering rain quickened, covering the newly roused forest with spring despair. The jackdaws fell silent and disappeared somewhere beyond the little village in the tall unripe rye and barley.

"Major, may I know the reasons why you've attached yourself to my party?"

He cast you a glance from beneath his grizzled brows. "Maybe it's a lark, maybe penance for my sins. What difference can it make to you?"

Just then you saw the captain of the rear guard, a tall, valiant young man carrying a double-barreled shotgun and a large lancer's saber, racing down the middle of the high road. He rushed up to you and the major and, his voice cracking with emotion, reported directly, forgetting regulations entirely. "Muscovites, lots of them, behind us."

"How close?"

"How do I know, a verst, a verst and a half."

"Are they in a marching column?"

"I didn't get that close a look. They keep coming out of the forest and going back in."

You drew your pistol from your belt. It was so quiet that you heard the single screech of a crane which had bent over a well out of sight at the edge of a village. The rebels froze in uncertain expectation.

"Call assembly. We're moving out."

A moment later, the mournful sound of a hunter's horn rang out. Ardent and eager, the rebels formed up on the high road now wet with rain. The rain was beating down faster as if hurrying to the aid of the pursued.

"My boy," said the major, "I don't know who taught you the art of war, but in my opinion there isn't enough forest for all this running around. What are we, cowards, ants? Let's make a stand in the village and blast the Muscovites. You'll see, they'll turn tail right away."

"Major," you said threateningly, "you are under my command. Take charge of the forward guard and begin marching immediately toward Rosoliszki."

"It's not for the likes of us to bargain for butter, there's the servants for that," answered Nawalkiewicz with a Belorussian proverb. He straightened his odd hunter's cap on his red, bald head and set off toward the village, moving to the head of the column.

You marched down the winding high road through the drab, blurred forest. By then all of you were soaked with rain and there was an air of fatigue about the hunched bodies of your men. When the head of the column halted for a moment in front of some obstacle and the tramping of feet ceased, you heard the distant song of soldiers, the wild Asiatic thunder of a Russian church choir. It was not all that long ago that you, too, had sung such songs in the Petersburg military school under the distracted eye of the Tsar, there observing forced maneuvers.

And so you listened with a quickened heart to that distant singing, which both attracted and repelled you. Suddenly you were seized by panic at the battle which had to happen, which would happen in the next few hours, for the Muscovites would never let you out of their sight, they would follow you to hell itself. That battle—the crackle of gunfire, the stink of gunpowder, the oppressive sudden easiness of death. Men would deprive each other of life, that gift from nature or heaven. For a brief moment you were astounded by the finality of the clash, the battle, the killing. You wondered what tomorrow would be like, a year, thirty years from tomorrow. Whether you'd exist at all or whether you'd be swallowed up by a purgatory you dimly understood or by the nothingness you'd always suspected, the black void of non-being.

The head of the column began moving. On your way to the rear you stepped in a large, deep, wavy puddle. Someone was walking behind you, breathing hoarsely.

"Karnowski," you said without turning around.

"Yes, sir."

"How many soldiers are behind us?"

"Looks like about a hundred."

"That could be. One division. We're outnumbered two to one. Are you feeling sick, Karnowski?"

"Yes, in my chest. But it's nothing. I've had it for years, I'm used to it."

"You'll rest in the new Polish state, Karnowski."

"Yes, we'll rest then, Colonel."

Suddenly the high road broke off and you came out

onto a narrow causeway made of old, rotted-out logs, so narrow your soldiers had to walk single file. On either side the eternal marshes, frightening, bottomless, overgrown with sickly grasses and broken by the trunks of dead trees. In the cadaverous white mist the herons stood stock-still, like clay Kermis figurines. Black and putrid, the marsh waters slurped and gurgled greedily beneath your feet.

Now your heart truly began ringing like a bell. Your pulse throbbed at your temples. You raised your head to catch a few sterile drops of water for your parched throat. Your fate as a young military commander was being decided. The fate of your war was being decided.

"Go up front," you whispered to the soldier walking in front of you. "Halt at the end of the dam and await orders."

The path through the marshes was less than a kilometer long. Soon you were on drier ground where the forest high road resumed. A few soldiers sank helplessly in the watery moss.

"Major, come here, please!" you called out.

Looking like a sopping-wet scarecrow, Major Nawalkiewicz appeared before you, wearing the enemy's overcoat, his shotgun slung upside down to keep the rain out.

"Major, we're going to do battle. You and your men will take the left side, I'll take the right. The Muscovites have to cross that dam single file, just as we did. Our gunners will have an excellent target. It's a heaven-sent opportunity. This will make a good beginning for us. A victorious skirmish will raise morale, and not only in our detachment. So, are you ready, Major?"

"You're a sly one. Well, you may as well give it a try, anyway. But did you hear them singing? Ach, they've got good song leaders. Sends chills up your spine."

"Major, God forbid anyone fires a shot before I give

the command. We have to let them approach as close as possible. We'll open fire when the trumpet sounds—I mean, the horn. Do you understand?"

"What's there to understand, my lad? They know we'll be waiting for them at the end of the dam."

"So, please take up your position, and Godspeed to you." Another nasty, ominous shudder shook your body.

"We'll live, we'll see," he sighed. "The worst of it's, my tooth's started hurting me."

"Major, just please await the signal from the horn."

"I know, I know, Colonel. I don't need any lessons from you."

Close by, beneath a spreading maple tree, stood the standard-bearer holding his standard still unfurled; large shimmering drops fell from its edging. Inseparable from his standard Ildek stood guard beside it, holding his old fowling piece with such passionate intensity that his fingers had turned white.

"Roll up that standard," you ordered. "Ildek, are you a good shot?"

"None better around here," bragged the youth. "I can hit a mosquito at a hundred paces, Colonel."

"In that case, go over to the other side with the major. Just find yourself a good hiding place in the trees. I don't want any of my men to be seen."

"We're all hunters here, Colonel," said the standard-bearer indulgently. "We know."

"Too bad there's no more wine," added Ildek. "My hands are numb."

"We mustn't get our courage from wine. To your positions, men."

Once again you were seized by an attack of trembling. You fell down onto the grass holding your face in your burning hands. From the mist, rain, and sloth of the dead-silent forest the alien sound bored its way through to you, that sound like the howling of wolves.

Oh, God, let us win, you whispered into the palms of your hands trickling with warm raindrops. So that all this need not be in vain. So that my life, the suffering and sacrifice of so many people . . . Oh, God, God Almighty . . .

A shot rang out and its echo wandered through the forest for a long moment. The soldiers had reached the dam. They were all jumbling up together at the edge, not daring to set foot on the narrow path through the marshes. You heard their cries and calls, the metallic click of bayonets being fixed to rifles, non-coms growling commands. Still, for some reason, no one was eager to attack. Indifferent to the bloody spectacle, the herons flapped up from the bogs and sailed majestically over the misty wall of the forest.

At that very moment a year-old dead maple seed fell in front of you, the kind children call "nosies," and split open and paste on their noses in springtime. That little golden wing had flown from a great height, twirling frantically; it had sailed an unusually long time, unable to reach the ground now saturated with rain.

Finally a few enemy soldiers set out on the black path across the dam. They walked reluctantly, dragging their feet, stopping every so often to shout something back to those who had remained behind. A few more soaked, hunched figures barbed with bayonets slipped out onto the path. They, too, did not move eagerly, both wanting and not wanting to attack. You and your men were waiting hidden behind trees, each aware of the pounding of his frantic blood.

More soldiers stepped out onto the causeway, where they clustered together in little groups discussing something. From time to time one of them would shoot into the forest, the contemptuously silent, indifferent forest dripping with rain.

Finally, three daredevils drew closer, now about two hundred paces from you, knelt down on the rotted beams, and aimed their rifles in your direction. You raised your hand to signal the trumpeter. The horn's first note was not particularly brave, but then it spoke loud and clear, becoming a command. One of your soldiers fired from your end of the causeway. Then, through the fading reverberations of gunfire, you heard the inhuman, terrifying yelp of a dying man, the headlong stamping of feet, the cracking of broken branches, and cries full of terror—Run! Run!

The soldiers on the causeway took to their heels as well. They ran as fast as they could back to their part of the forest. In the twinkling of an eye an entire company had vanished into the uniform gray mist. It had grown so quiet you could hear the distant chatter of a stork settling down in its nest.

"Karnowski, come here!" you called out in a subdued voice.

But no one appeared, no one answered. Raindrops were spattering the lilac bushes. The first wind had sprung up, a northeasterly wind, the sort which blights a premature spring with light frost.

You shuddered and rose from the icy ground. None of your rebels was near you behind the trees and you went out onto the high road.

"Major, Major, what happened?"

The wind sank lower. The trees bent with an exalted rustling like an angry choir pronouncing a curse. You sprang to the other side of the road, stumbling on an abandoned gun still warm from someone's hands. You stopped abruptly and suddenly grew terribly cold. There was a dead man before you lying in a broken bush. It was Ildefons, the boy in the long fur coat, the youngest rebel.

He was lying on his back with outflung arms, his fingers grasping dry oak leaves, two handfuls of leaves, as if he were about to toss them in your face. A large bullethole shone redly above his left eyebrow.

"Men!" you called. "Where are you! I'm calling you in the name of God!"

No rebels, no Russians. Only the forest busy with its own affairs, the forest roaring like a mill, and the drifting autumn mist. You started running down the impassable trails beside the high road. Abandoned weapons lay everywhere; double-barreled shotguns, sabers, revolvers, cartridges. Near an uprooted tree you saw the standard and beside it a black cap tossed away to facilitate escape. Everyone had fled, from a single shot. Both the attackers and the attacked. I, too, experienced a moment like that and perhaps, if I remember rightly, even several such moments, filled with strange terror.

You returned to Ildefons, fighting back the increasing spasms of what was either fever or common tears. You closed his gaping eyes and his mouth, whose teeth now seemed somehow enlarged, and placed his still-warm hands across his chest. He lay there helpless, drenched. You covered him with a large branch of flowering bird cherry and then he lay buried in the vast, foul closeness of the small white flowers.

The wind was scattering the clouds, revealing a sky suffused with red. The evil day was over. Once again a lovely night lit by distant galaxies was drawing near. You gathered up the abandoned weapons, picked up the wet, heavy standard, and dragged all of it off to a huge hollow in an ancient oak tree. You hid your own sword there as well but kept Sulistrowski's revolver. Thus ended your campaign in the year 1863.

You dozed through the entire night on your feet like a heron, beneath a tree which sighed and moaned, buffeted by the wind. Every so often, old friends and enemies emerged from the forest wanting something from you, cursing you for something, threatening you with something, disappearing for a moment only once again to crawl out from behind uprooted trees and reach out to you with clutching hands. Among them you saw your father and colonels from the St. Petersburg Engineering School, your sister in mourning and Turkish guards, colleagues from Genoa and the priest who taught catechism, French Zouaves and Garibaldi. Your entire short life pressed itself on you from every side. Your entire small universe was making terrible, atrocious claims on you which could neither be averted nor annulled.

From time to time you were wakened by your own groaning. Little by little you remembered your cruel fate, your utter defeat. The fate and defeat of yet another generation in the tragic pilgrimage of many generations of Poles. Somewhere near you in the darkness Ildefons the zealous slept in eternal sleep: Ildek, whose mother had sewn him an unfashionable coat. Myopic, distracted, the stars looked down from the sky.

Finally the darkness began to sink into the sopping earth. As if torn from a nightmare a crane cried in the marshes. The first familiar trees appeared. A belated evening cloud glowed in the center of the sky.

You broke off a stick from the branch of a tree and, driven by the rain, set off toward Rosoliszki. You stumbled as you walked, tripping on misshapen roots, those petrified veins of the forest, until finally, at the end of the forest, you saw a substantial little house with windows and a chimney issuing a thin, straight line of smoke. Not far away Rosoliszki, covered by curls of vernal green, was waking to the day.

You pushed open the door to a hallway redolent of mushrooms and walked into a spacious kitchen with an enormous stove in the left-hand corner. Three young women wearing flaxen shirts and skirts were bustling about the stove, flushed from the heat and their labors. They were removing ash-covered coals from the earthen stove to ready a place for large, lustrous loaves of bread marked deeply with signs of the cross. Through their open shirts you saw their heavy, handsome breasts covered with a fine gleam of delicate sweat. You drank in this timeless domestic activity, which brought back touching memories, while they, busy with their work, did not notice you. Finally, sparks flew up from a mound of oak coals and they jumped back to a spot on the earthen floor lit by the hazy light of the rising sun.

It was then that they saw you.

"Praised be Jesus Christ," you managed to say.

"World without end," replied the oldest girl.

"I request your hospitality. I am traveling and much in need of food."

They looked you over, exchanged glances; then the youngest, who was clearly the mistress of the house, said in a singsong voice, "So then be seated at our table. Breakfast will be ready right away."

It cost you some effort to sit yourself down on the old bench by the window. The young one with the snub nose squinted curiously in your direction.

"And where are you traveling to, sir?" she asked, pouring dough into a large iron frying pan.

"Nowogrodok," you answered after a moment's thought.

"A long way. Breakfast will be ready in a minute, so you can have a nice bite to eat and something for your thirst, sir. We get up with the sun, the forest loves the morning, and our men work in the forest."

The older girls shoved the loaves of sour-smelling bread into the dark interior of the stove while the young one made pancakes on the cooling embers. From beneath the eaves of the house came the cries of quarrelsome swallows.

"You're shaking from fever," the oldest remarked benevolently.

"It's nothing. It's from not sleeping. I lost my way in the forest."

"The forest's dangerous these days, especially if you're traveling alone."

"I'm not afraid of being robbed."

"Perhaps not of being robbed, but there are other dangers."

You fell silent, to avoid a touchy subject. A large cat with dark stripes jumped down from the stove, stretched and yawned luxuriously, then walked over to you and rubbed against your legs.

"Look, he liked the stranger right off," said the young one in surprise.

She smiled at you with a child's impudence, saying to the cat, "Vashka, Vashka, where have you been, who have you been drinking milk with?"

Feeling your eyes on them, the handsome young women began moving with dancelike grace. When they giggled, their embroidered shirts were pulled tight over their breasts, but you did not need that sight to sense their warm, pulsing blood and their bodies redolent of river water beneath the coarse cloth. I, too, longed for their lovely, mysterious bodies on those autumn nights in 1944 when we drank home brew in the hay, while they, hidden by the night, sang those piercing songs, songs like wailing, like laments, songs like a terrible longing for something without a name. I cannot resist remembering Emilka, flaxen-haired, ashen-haired, silver-haired Emilka, with a complexion like an autumn apple or July honey or perhaps rather like smoky heather, no, not that either, better to say with a skin and complexion that cannot be described at all, but whose quiver, luster, and delicate pulsations drove me mad; you, too, were deprived of your reason, for they have always lived on this earth, in country houses, backwaters, and villages lost in the forest, those golden, rosy Emilkas whom you dream of till the end of your days.

Then the young one, who could also have been an Emilka, brought you a large oatmeal pancake in the frying pan and flipped it into your clay bowl. A piece of melted salt bacon sizzled in another pot. You tore off a piece of pancake, rolled it up, and were about to dip it into the fat when suddenly three woodsmen walked into the kitchen. In silence they set their hatchets down in the corner, in silence they looked over at you as you battled a sudden weariness, a piece of hot pancake in your dirty fingers.

"A traveler. Going to Nowogrodok," the young one who could have been Emilka said quickly.

Saying nothing, they joined you at the table. There was an air of fatigue and the odor of resin about them; they seemed to be staring down at the gnarled table, but you sensed they were observing you. Reluctantly you bit off a piece of pancake, slightly dry now but with a drop of golden fat on it.

"Dangerous to wander around in clothes like that," said a dark-haired woodsman with large sorrowful eyes.

"The clothes wouldn't matter if the weather was good," you answered with studied courtesy.

"It's a dangerous time, too," added the dark-haired woodsman. "It's not a normal year, things are strange, people are angry as wolves."

"I'm going to my relatives to help with the harvest," you said with an alacrity which even struck you as suspect.

The dark-haired woodsman looked at you or through you at the opaque window, whose glass was scarred by frozen air bubbles. Then Emilka walked quietly over to you, stroked your hair and forehead with her warm hand as if taking a sick man into her protection against the men, the evil hour, the uncertainties of life.

"A man can't change the world," said the dark-haired woodsman, fixing on some memory obscured by pain. "Man is born to suffer. Pain, nothingness. I lost my cap in the woods. I have to go back and look for it."

"Eat your pancake, it's getting cold," interjected Emilka.

"No, first we have to find what's been lost, wife."

He rose from the table and started for the door. He stopped at the threshold, looked back at you, hesitated a moment, then finally ran out of the house, startling away a large flock of sparrows.

"He's a good person," said Emilka gently. "His life is hard. He suffers, he cries at night, but he's a good, kind soul. He spent his whole youth in Siberia."

"Why was he sent there?" you asked, stunned by the fever battering every fiber of your stiff muscles.

"Who knows." Emilka stroked your dry, springy hair automatically. At that time, like myself, you had a great shock of bushy hair dry as spring hay. "He never talks about it. Sometimes just before dawn he screams and wakes up and doesn't say a word till the sun rises."

"A wandering beggar prophesied that I would live in a distant southern land where the sun never sets."

"What God gives, that will be," said a bearded woodsman, staring at his bowl of cracklings. "A person can live anywhere. Everyone's life is all written up there." He pointed up at the ceiling and the rain-washed spring sky.

"Eat, young man, eat; you'll get better, you'll go see your sweetheart," whispered Emilka.

You felt her warmth mixed with the smell of smoke on your temples.

"My sweetheart," you mumbled as if in a fever-dazed dream. "My sweetheart is Poland, golden-haired Poland, bloody, enslaved."

"What are you talking about?" The bearded woodsman leaned over the table.

The door opened. The dark-haired woodsman with the mournful eyes stood in the doorway, his broad shoulders screening two peasants, one of whom had reins or a tether coiled around one shoulder. They entered the hut cautiously, the peasants piously removing their raggedy sheepskin caps.

The woodsman took a roll of stiff paper from inside his shirt, unrolled it, and, with a pain-contorted smirk, asked you, "Can you read this to us?"

"Are you really illiterate?" you said, raising your roaring head with difficulty.

"We're all illiterate here. But this has to be read, it was sent from Oszmiana."

For a moment you looked into his eyes full of pain and anger, sadness and hatred, fear and indifference.

"The peasants are asking you a favor. It's a government paper. Read it to them, then be on your way."

Against your will you rose from the bench. The women closed the stove's cast-iron cover. There was a telltale trail of sweet-smelling coal smoke near the ceiling. Suddenly the hut and the people standing dead still began to sway, the floor began running down and away, and you had to grab hold of the table's slippery edge.

"Give me the paper," you said with a sudden, incomprehensible fear.

He passed you the rectangle of paper, its ink still sticky. The letters hopped about before your eyes, but you overcame the wild chaos of fever and began to make out individual words in the tangled ink.

To the peasants of the Western Provinces of the Empire:
In connection with the disturbances provoked by rebelliously
inclined individuals, and in connection with the disorders
occurring in certain counties, and in connection with the
protests brought before the throne by loyal subjects, and on
the basis of the Highest Order, I command all peasants to
take an active part in combatting all and any displays of
criminal rebellion. The following must be apprehended and
delivered over to the military authorities without delay—all
individuals bearing arms both in the forest and in the
countryside, all unknown persons not in possession of trust-
worthy documents, as well as suspicious persons no matter
who they are. I am establishing the following rewards
for malefactors apprehended: for an unarmed man, three
rubles . . .

You broke off reading and raised your eyes from the
handbill. They were standing in front of you looking ready
to spring. Somewhere in the meadows near Rosoliszki a
shepherd was singing in a mournful, yearning falsetto:
"Hey, Hala, Hala, you young girl . . ." You tried to swallow
the saliva trapped in your constricted throat.

"Keep reading, sir, about how the governor's giving
rewards to poor people."

"Damn you!" you were about to whisper, thrusting
your hand inside your coat for your pistol.

But they were too quick. They sprang at you from all
sides like wolves; in a flash they'd thrown you to the
earthen floor and tied you with the reins like a ram.
Somewhere in the distance you heard the muffled cries of
women, the desperate sobs of your Emilka, who perhaps
tried to defend you, the furious shouts of the peasants or
the woodsmen; then everything grew quiet, soft, blank, as
if you'd been immersed in water warmed by the sun.

Later a piercing pain in your back brought you to
consciousness again. Your hands had been twisted behind
you and roped with peasant thoroughness like the shaft

bow of a cart. The two villagers were ransacking your pockets under the sullen eye of the woodsman. They pulled out your pistol, gold watch, money, insurgency documents, and notes. The woodsman examined them with unusual skill and set them down on the table.

"Take the watch and the money. They're worth more than the reward," you moaned.

"You rebelled against your own fate," said the woodsman. "You'll get the punishment awaiting you."

"A terrible curse will fall on your head and on the heads of everyone from this place."

"God ordained the powers that be. It's not for us sinners to overthrow His decrees."

"But didn't you, too, once suffer as I'm suffering now?"

"Take the colonel out. Let him have a last look at the sky and the forest," ordered the woodsman.

They dragged you through the dark passageway to a porch overgrown with bindweed. The small violet flowers had already closed in fear of the intrusive sun. The shepherd was still singing his nostalgic song about Hala.

Beside the road stood a wagon surrounded by soldiers who might have been Chechens from the distant Caucasus. Two Cossacks were having trouble restraining their horses tormented by gadflies.

Covered with dry dung, the team started toward the porch and stopped in front of you. The two peasants were holding you. Reining their fidgety mounts, the Cossacks jumped onto the wagon. One of them wore the badge of a commander.

"Go on, lad." One of the peasants elbowed you in the back.

They led you down from the porch. The other man, a common settlement Cossack, rode his horse straight at you, and when you staggered out of the way, he lashed you across the forehead with his knout. The top of your head suddenly began to feel hot and itchy but you couldn't scratch it because your hands were tied behind your back.

Taking a deep breath to summon strength, the peasants tossed you up onto the wagon and then, with an economic sense of detail, began tying your legs to the wagon stakes.

Some dark-eyed soldiers, no doubt Chechens, came running up, their overcoats unbuttoned.

"Hey, rebel, I fuck your mother," rasped one of them, and slammed his rifle butt in your ribs. The other one directed a surprise blow at your unprotected throat. You groaned, gurgling, hiding your face in the hollow of your collarbone.

"In Wilno there'll be a trial and a gallows, understand?" asked an old non-com with a drooping gray mustache. He watched you closely, curious to see your reaction. But all you felt was the roaring beneath the band of your ribs and that hot throbbing which split your itching skull. Through the slits of your swollen eyelids you saw a strip of road and a wooden roadside cross; a bent, unhappy figure who seemed to be Karnowski passed that moss-covered cross on some mysterious journey. I, too, used to have apparitions of my own Karnowski, whom for no particular reason I had remembered from childhood.

The Cossack commander looked down at you from the height of his small, thin horse. As if speaking to his prisoner but probably really to himself, he recited softly some famous lines from Pushkin, the greatest poet of the eastern Slavs:

> *Once again our standards have broken through*
> *the breaches of Warsaw fallen once again:*
> *And Poland like a regiment in flight*
> *flings its bloody banner to the dust*
> *and mutiny returns to silence, crushed . . .*

He raised his hand, giving the signal to move out. The soldiers surrounded the wagon closely, the peasants clucked at the horses. Arduously you turned your head around in a senseless desire to see the woodsman's cottage, and the encouraging sight of bright smoke streaming straight up into the spring blue of the sky. You saw the woodsman who had turned you in. He was looking at your ill-treated body, your legs spread shamefully like those of a gutted boar, streaks of blood clinging to your forehead like leeches. He whispered something. His eyes were moist, there was an uncertainty in his voice as he moved his numb lips, but you, my brother across these eighty years, read on the woodsman's twitching lips that question which is always with us:

"Was it worth it?"

*
*   *

Nothing new back in line. Though it was a bit more ragged, and a few people were in different spots. The meager light of the candles dripping their wax tears made people look grotesque and gave the weary faces an unnatural appearance. Iwona's large, protruding eyes looked at us, or perhaps at me, as we knocked the clumps of snow from our boots at the entrance to the shop.

The store manager and a man wearing a black apron were carrying in the first cardboard box. The line crowded together and pressed against the counter, on which there was a sign: PLEASE DO NOT LEAN ON COUNTER. I recognized Iwona's handwriting, though I had never seen that Mediterranean girl's writing before in my life.

"Where was I standing? Where's my place?" whined the peasant woman; her enormous bundle had been strapped to her for several hours.

Everyone maintained a silent, vigilant indifference.

"Step over here," said the manager, indicating the head of the line.

"Hey," said a construction worker in the line. "What's going on here?"

"Can't you see this person is from out of town," replied the manager coldly, straightening some drooping hair with a large red fingernail.

"Don't let people in! Watch it!" people were shouting from the end of the line.

The line closed ranks, pressing against the glass counter; the little candle flames trembled in fear. The manager broke open the cardboard box, plunged in her hands, and began groping, still keeping a stern and bloodshot eye on us. She rustled, shuffled her feet, squinted, and stuck out her tongue; her body grew taut, as if she was about to pull something from the box, but she slipped and fell back with a handful of wood shavings.

Those standing closest helped her up and asked with concern, "What's in there? Tell us."

"Strange," said the manager, shaking her head.

"Gold?"

"Probably silver."

"Maybe silver on top and gold under?"

"Start pulling the goddamn stuff out, we're losing patience here," roared Duszek.

The manager rolled up her sleeves and wriggled her fingers like a surgeon before an operation.

"Give me some light, girl," she said over her shoulder.

Iwona picked up a candle and approached her boss, her eyes looking out over the line of heads at the shop window dusted with snow. By some inexplicable chance a solitary snowflake fell from the ceiling, heading right for the candle's flame. Iwona caught it with the candle and listened for a moment to the painful sizzle.

"Not over there, bring the light here," the manager said in a tone of instruction.

Finally she bent over the box and plunged her arms in up to the elbow. Panting, shifting from foot to foot, she tensed herself and pulled out a clattering lustrous object still tied in its wrappings.

"Silver!" cried the woman in the pelisse in a voice somewhere between triumph and despair.

"The hell with silver," growled Kojran. "Hurry it up, sweetheart, it's almost Christmas Eve."

The manager raised the shining object and set it on the glass counter.

"A samovar. A Soviet electric samovar," someone stated deadpan.

"For God's sake, it's samovars and we've been standing here since this morning!" the construction worker burst out in despair.

"Keep looking, sweetheart, check all the cases."

The manager and the man in the apron went to the back of the store and returned a moment later to say, "Unfortunately, they're all samovars."

The crowd surged against the counter. I, too, surged forward, though I suddenly felt short of breath.

"But they were supposed to bring gold!" I roared.

"There's nothing I can do about it."

"Get on the phone. It's a gyp. We've been waiting a week, I'm leaving tomorrow," raged Kojran.

"Is this how you treat workers, you bitch?" threatened the construction worker.

Only the anarchist and the student remained calm; they clung to the counter, guarding their place in line.

"Maybe there'll be another delivery?" asked the peasant woman timidly; her kerchief had slipped from her head, revealing a fashionable holiday hairstyle straight from London.

"They may make a second delivery," concurred the manager. "They promised it for today. Who'd like a nice modern samovar? They're very much in demand."

"You know what you can do with that samovar," cursed the construction worker.

Duszek smiled cunningly. "Kojran, buy one, don't be so stingy. You can use it in America; one whiff and you'll think of home. You're the sentimental type."

"Fine for you to make jokes. But I'm leaving tomorrow. What am I going to do with all my Polish money?"

"Let's wait a while. Maybe they'll make another delivery, since they promised," I said.

"What do you want to buy?"

"Rings. Wedding rings," I answered.

"Getting married in your old age?"

"God forbid."

"So what do you need wedding rings for?"

"No reason."

"What do you mean, no reason? You spend good money on nonsense without any reason? You could be buying diamonds, so then why gold rings and not something else?"

"I can't buy diamonds and I can't buy rings because they didn't deliver either."

"Now that's true."

Kojran stealthily opened the zipper of his shoulder bag and seemed to be looking for something.

"Making sure the cash box hasn't been robbed?" I asked with a sneer.

"Mind your own."

A couple who looked like government office workers gave up their place in line and departed, cursing socialist business. Through the momentarily open door a blast of snow blew in, along with the sounds of a carol being played somewhere nearby, by the veterans' band. The peasant woman disentangled herself from her kerchief and canvas bag as if from a uniform no longer needed. Only then could we see she was wearing a worn but still elegant caracul coat. She stopped near us, holding a small flat flask in one hand and in the other some metal glasses.

"You won't refuse, will you, gentlemen?"

"Thank you," I said. "It's been a lousy day."

"He always says that," growled Kojran. "So he can be the center of attention."

The woman filled three of the little glasses, their gold signets gleaming. The man dressed in denim edged over to us with an ingratiating smile.

"Maybe you could find an extra drop for me? My name is Grzesio."

"You're a spy, son," said Duszek sullenly.

"I don't understand, what are you getting at?"

"I was working that trade before you'd seen daylight."

"I have no idea what you're talking about."

"Just drink and forget about us."

Iwona walked over to the window. She blew on the glass and traced a word with her finger on the light-blue mist. My breastbone was hurting again. I felt cold and short of breath at the same time.

"You complain about the lines while drinking whiskey," remarked the woman in the pelisse ironically.

"Now you're going to tell us people stand in lines in America, too," growled Kojran.

"Naturally they do. All you see here are the short-comings."

"Do you people know the joke about the Party Secretary?" interjected Grzesio.

"All right, all right, don't be feeling us out, we don't go for that." Duszek scowled.

Kojran shook the last of his drink from the nickel cup.

"Wait a second, wait a second, Konwa, do you remember the bajstruk?"

"I seem to remember something."

"You always seem to remember something, but never more than you need to. Why don't you remember things fully and accurately?"

"Why don't I remember things fully and accurately? That really is a problem."

"I'll do the remembering and remind you about the bajstruk. A beast the size of a goat, sometimes even larger. Had three legs, the fourth was hidden. His face looked like a teddy bear's, or sometimes like an owl's. He ate mushrooms, grass, bark, but he didn't scorn field mice or hares, either. You don't remember the bajstruk, Konwa?"

"I saw one once toward the end of the war. From a distance, though."

"He lived in the forests—in Nabolicka woods, Ruska, Nadniemenska. A forester ran into one even in Rudnicka. People said the bajstruk was wiser than men. Sometimes he would save people who had lost their way and lead them to a village. He saved a child from a wolf. In the winter he warmed an old man with the heat of his own body. But God forbid you run into one on a moonlit night. They know how to suck a person's blood, bite a stray horse to death, or burn down a barn full of grain. Am I telling it right, Konwa?"

"Who's supposed to believe that?" Duszek sniggered hoarsely. "You're dreaming again. All you people from Lithuania are a bit touched. And of course you've been kicked by that bajstruk of yours."

"He had eyes like a man. But larger, sad, more knowing. He used that hidden fourth leg to kill, when he had to kill."

"So what happened to it? You never see anything

about it in the papers or on television, either," scoffed Duszek.

Kojran leaned his elbows on the glass counter and looked with a dolorous gaze at the semi-precious stones from the Urals in their velveteen boxes.

"The Nazis wiped them out."

"Not even one pair survived?"

"Maybe. Nobody knows."

I unbuttoned my sheepskin coat. It had become hard to breathe again. Iwona broke a thin icicle off the frame of the display window as she sucked on it, and fine circles of vapor emanated from her mouth.

"Kojran," I said, "why are you going to America? You know, one day you'll go to bed and start shivering as if you were running a fever and then you'll start whining about how you have to come back home. You'll be overcome by strange fears, and before you know it you'll be wishing you were in line at a jewelry store where people just stand and worry and wait—by the way, just what are we waiting for?"

"You're waiting for a miracle and I'm waiting for Soviet rings."

"I'd swap my whole goddamned life for three rings and plunge into a brand-new world."

The woman in the pelisse was looking in a mirror, adjusting her overlarge hat. "It's probably so cold in America, even the oldest old people can't remember anything like it."

Kojran fixed his gaze on her for a long moment. "And it doesn't get cold here?"

"You've gotten used to complaining."

"Duszek, do I complain?"

"Sometimes you do."

"When a Pole complains, he feels better right away."

"Who said that?" Duszek thrust his cold face menacingly out from his collar.

"Me," answered Grzesio.

"Where'd you learn such golden thoughts?"

"From you."

Duszek gathered himself up, released a cloud of vapor, and sighed: "You'll go far. Maybe farther than me."

Neon lights went on outside, illuminating Iwona, who was standing by the window, then blinked out. Outlined in blood-red light, she had looked like something from another world. From the depths of the snow-covered city, barely audible music filtered in to us. The veterans' band was working, strumming patriotic Christmas carols and Christmas-carol patriotism.

"What if I just walked over to Iwona and proposed marriage to her?" asked Kojran in a whisper.

"She's dreaming about something. She's somewhere else."

"I'll show her my passport. I'll show her a handful of bills with Washington's picture, I'll show her a snapshot of the gas station with the church for all the religions over it. That'd be a beginning. Are you married?"

"I am. I have two daughters."

"Disgraceful. How bourgeois. Konwa, you're a petit bourgeois pretending to be a romantic."

"Do you have a wife?"

"I had a few. They all left me. But I'd try one more time."

"You're such a great guy, but they leave you. You want to be the judge of me but you don't even know how to stick it in right."

"I am your judge. I've read everything you ever dished up. I have a bookshelf where I keep you under lock and key, because your work is such a fleeting thing. It hangs on the thread of the moment. You are a temporary writer. Your books will die with you."

"Shhh, don't say that so loud. I have a wife and children."

"Are you trying to make fun of me? I don't have a low opinion of you. A sense of the moment is a gift from God, too. That readiness to latch on to whatever's hot. You burn your hands but you do your work. People buy your books, read them, discuss them. A total illusion of authenticity."

"Say something about my cleverness. I know you're saving the best for last."

"See, Konwa, you know yourself. Your cleverness is not the meager cunning of the passing pen pusher, those failures who whine, flatter, brown-nose, scrape, bluff, screw influential wives, screw the regime from behind, screw high society and foreign circles. Your cleverness is that of a minister of police, a great provocateur who wants to die on the cross. Your cleverness is vile, elusive, exalted, dripping with sincerity, a foul sentimental attempt at sanctity aspiring to the tragic. Your cleverness is such that its every gleam kills you forever, for all time. Your books aren't kosher and nobody will ever touch them again."

"I wish it were so. You're flattering me before leaving on a long trip which frightens you."

"You really don't remember the bajstruk?"

"It's just a dream you had on this magical day before Christmas. If there had been bajstruks around Wilno, they'd have been other places, too."

"And if an earthquake happens in one country, does another one have to have one, too? The Soviets caught the last bajstruk when they entered Wilno in '44. They shipped it off to Alma-Ata, to a zoo in Central Asia. When a bajstruk bit someone, it was curtains. He licked a leper and his health returned."

From outside I could hear the monotonous song of trolley cars stuck in snowdrifts and, closer to us, the un-hurried shuffling of feet, the prisoners beginning to scrape away the snow. Iwona sat down in her chair, laid her open book on her lap, unable to read because of the darkness. She placed her fingers on the cold pages, closed her eyes, and either read using her fingers or else sank into lethargy, the lethargy of the afternoon of the day before Christmas. No, she was simply ignoring us. She was testing her tele-pathic connection with a world of her own, her native planet. That's the version I preferred.

The manager returned from the rear of the store car-rying some sort of official paper. She walked up to a candle and removed her glasses with their coquettishly tinted lenses. The line grew still and instinctively closed ranks near the front of the counter.

"Your attention, please, ladies and gentlemen," said the manager. "I have received a memo from our adminis-tration informing our dear customers of a surprise bonus. If you make a purchase in any of our stores, keep your sales slip. We will be giving away five trips to the Soviet Union to customers with lucky sales slips."

"But where's the goods?" shouted the construction worker insolently.

"There's plenty of merchandise. Please look around and see what strikes you."

"There were supposed to be Soviet rings!"

"And precious stones!"

The manager folded up the official paper. "I can't make them appear out of thin air, you realize. The van has already left. Perhaps it's gotten stuck in a snowdrift. You can see yourselves what it's like out."

Suddenly there was a click of a spring and a flash of cadaverous blue light, like a sudden bolt of lightning. A scuffle broke out in the middle of the store.

"Give me that camera," snarled the denim-clad Grzesio, ripping the camera from the fat, red-bearded anarchist.

"Sorry, sorry, sorry," repeated the anarchist, struggling furiously with his assailant.

"Hand over the film or I'll call the police."

"Jesus and Mary, he took our picture!" wailed the woman in the pelisse.

"What, taking pictures isn't allowed?" said the student, defending the anarchist. "Where is that written?"

"It's written where it's supposed to be. Now hand over that film and right now, or I'll take you outside."

The woman in the pelisse joined in. She grabbed the French ex-terrorist by the waist. "Manager, manager, he was taking pictures!"

"In principle taking pictures is not permitted," said the manager in consternation. "And what did he photograph?"

"Us. The whole line."

"We weren't asked."

"That's the point," interjected the peasant woman.

The student broke up the fight. He shielded the besieged foreigner with his own anemic person. "This is disgraceful! What's he going to think of us?"

"Let him think what he wants, as long as he hands over the film. Next they'll be printing it in some foreign newspaper. And who'll answer for that?" fumed the woman in the pelisse.

The Frenchman muttered, fiddling furiously with the camera. The shutter clicked again. Instinctively the construction workers covered their faces.

"He says," translated the student, "that he just overexposed the picture. He says that he wanted a souvenir photo, but if it's no, it's no. He loves Poland and wants to request Polish citizenship."

"And just what does he love us for?" asked Duszek suspiciously.

"Long live Poland!" The French anarchist attempted to raise a cheer.

"Quiet, quiet!" sputtered the manager. "Please keep the fuss down or I'll close the store for inventory."

"Poland has not yet perished," sang the Frenchman.

Meanwhile, I still was feeling short of breath. Inhaling the cold moisture with all my strength, I was suffocating from a lack of oxygen. The more greedily I sucked at the void, the more I died. I rushed blindly to the door, which did not want to yield. It had either frozen or been blocked by a snowdrift. At last with a piercing screech it gave way. I stumbled outside, seeing nothing but the silent whiteness gone gray now. The pain in my chest was receding. The air I gulped was becoming more substantial. I noticed dark windows in the snow-covered buildings, flocks of starlings flying past, and two guys far from sobriety trying to cross a high drift.

"Still, it's beautiful," piped up the legless cripple, who had settled himself on the summit of a pile of snow. He looked as if he were sinking luxuriously into a foamy bath. "The world is beautiful, you just have to know how to see it."

"And I'm dying."

"No wonder, all those hours in line. A tightness in the ribs, right?"

"Yes, and shortness of breath. Like being in a coffin, you know."

"I know, I know." The beggar laughed good-naturedly. "Take a look at your birth certificate. You couldn't run a hundred meters. Not that I'll be doing much running myself."

The prisoners were sitting in an elegant restaurant, drinking tea and casting derisive glances at the snow and the unfortunate pedestrians. A porter wearing bronze-colored livery was keeping an eye on their shovels which were leaning against the restaurant's marble façade.

"What do you think?" I asked all of a sudden.

"Think about what?"

"In general."

The beggar cleared one nostril, then the other. "I think we got walked over in this round."

"Are you thinking of our last round?"

"They cut off both my legs in the first round. In '44. You're suspicious, everybody's suspicious. Everybody thinks, Where did this jerk lose his legs? Maybe under a trolley car, maybe when he jumped from the fourth floor, or when he was sloshed to the gills. But I'll tell you the plain truth of it: It was in '44. Back then I was really something, beautiful, almost a saint. Poetic-type girls would kiss my stumps. I rose above degradation. No legs was like having four legs. A beautiful time it was. But now somehow that's all flown by. We won't be changing the world anymore."

"Over and done with. Perhaps forever? Perhaps fate has packed us off for a long trip into the depths of the universe? Would you like to sail off into infinity?"

"Over in Praga there's a certain carpenter. God and nature forgot all about him. He just lives, lives, goes on living, no end to it. Now he's starting to feel ashamed of having been passed over. In his youth he was a cooper, now he passes himself off as a carpenter, because who knows what a cooper is these days."

"No, ultimately there are no accidents. A combination of circumstances can cause you not to be born, but everybody has to die."

"I swear to God, go over to Praga. Everything is based on chance. Out of billions of identical fates, why can't there be one exception?"

"Ah, I don't feel like going over to Praga. I'm getting back in line."

*

I was molded from three different clays. And then fired in the temperate inferno of three elements. The clays were Polish, Lithuanian, and Belorussian, and the elements were Polishness, Russianness, and Judaism, or, more precisely, Jewishness.

An old story. There are many little nooks in Europe where diverse ethnic groups, various linguistic communities, variegated social and religious customs mingled without fusing. But that little niche of mine, the Wilno area, seems to me lovelier, better, more sublime and magical. Besides, I had labored hard to embellish the myth of that borderland of Europe and Asia, that ancient cradle of European nature and Asiatic demons, that flower-strewn valley of eternal harmony and human friendship.

I embellished the myth until I believed in that idealized land where love was more intense than anywhere else, where flowers were larger than in other countries, where people were more human than anywhere else in the whole world.

But really that enclave could not differ greatly from other such enclaves into which the nest of humanity, ancient Europe, had been divided. Exotic national and religious groups lived together on a small patch of land but no evangelical love thrived there. I would try to conceal the conflicts, animosities, and hatreds in which I had taken part and of which I was most sorely ashamed. And later on, when I had, after a fashion, mastered my pen, I strung our shared and incoherent fate on the fragile thread of human solidarity, friendship, and the magic of our common destiny.

There was a day, or a moment, at the very beginning of my flimsy literary career when I told myself that I would observe strictly only one commandment—Thou shalt not use thy words against foreigners. Thou shalt not use metaphors, emotional parables, or take a moral line against another person of another religion, another language. Thus, I have sinned against my own but not against strangers.

I steered myself toward universalism, one, naturally, which would include all humanity; I considered myself a carefully concealed cosmopolitan who, on the sly, tossed the sanctity of his own people onto the rubbish heap, who handed over the remnants of an epoch of religious and national strife to be ground in history's eternal mill.

With dread-filled amazement I leafed through patriotic stories written by my colleagues, and with a sense of pity I thumbed through works treating the sanctified martyrology of our own people. I was flying high. In the sterilized atmosphere of universal objectivism, I communed with man, with *Homo sapiens*, and it was only his soul, the soul of the species ruling the entire earth, which concerned me and beckoned me with inspiration.

One day, one moment, I read the first review which termed me a Polish writer, steeped in Polishness, confined to a Polish niche. I broke into hearty laughter at this obvious misunderstanding. I was, on principle, indifferent to the emotional, moral, or intellectual conditioning of the people from the devastated cities of the Vistula River. I came from a cosmopolitan Eden, from a sunken Atlantis, from an Ur-people, an Ur-language, an Ur-religion.

I stopped laughing later. My Polishness was being mentioned by all the critics. That Polishness had begun to turn against this ill-fated author. Because of that unwanted Polishness I became incomprehensible, monotonous, irritating. I began struggling against it in myself, I grew ashamed and afraid of it although I had never made any use of it, alluded to it, or even touched on it in thought. To me it was the most sin-laden of taboos. Of course, I had used certain true details, and depicted nature as I remembered it: varieties of trees, herbs, and moss which also grow in Belgium or Canada; I noted incidents from the war which could have occurred in Italy or Norway; I found psychological or moral deviations which could have described Germans or Americans as easily as Poles.

How did it happen that I am an author of Polish books, good or bad, but Polish? Why did I accept the role which I had renounced forever? Who turned me, a European, no, a citizen of the world, an Esperantist, a cosmopolitan, an agent of universalism, who turned me, as in some wicked fairy tale, into a stubborn, ignorant, furious Pole?

*

There was an idle calm in the jewelry store. A small group had formed around the student and the anarchist.

"They've lost interest over there in the West," interpreted the student. "They're tired of crisis. But he wants to dedicate his life to revolution."

"What revolution?" asked Grzesio.

"What do you mean, what revolution? Revolution in general. Wherever it's happening. That's why he came here."

"Does that mean we're going to have a revolution?" said Grzesio in surprise.

"A good provocateur"—Duszek smiled—"provokes nicely. He'll be tops in his trade."

"I didn't say there would be."

"So what did you say, then?"

"I could have said, for example, that we have an on-going revolution."

Grzesio took a long moment to ponder. He pulled a comb out of the pocket of his jeans and combed his thick, wavy hair.

"You're not talking straight."

"To me it seems suspicious that he comes here and loafs around in this cold," added the woman in the pelisse.

"And so you're standing in line for rings, too?" said Grzesio, picking up the thread. "He needs a signet ring for the revolution?"

"We're holding a place in line for a pensioner."

"How much's he paying you?"

"Two hundred."

"Cheap."

"Our prices aren't extravagant."

Duszek was listening with pleasure to this verbal fencing. Out of habit he sided with Grzesio, but in the end it was the thin, freezing student who won his sympathy.

"He's good, he's got an alibi."

A little lake of melting frost or ice had formed on the sill of a display window. Iwona took a thick candle and let the wax dribble into the shallow pond. She took a close look at the white figures, which formed blood-red traces of color frozen in the cold.

The peasant woman walked over to us discreetly, exuding Dior perfume. "Would you like another?" she asked.

"We shall not refuse," said Kojran with a bow.

"I'm thinking of giving up. I don't feel particularly well," I said.

"You're feeling bad? How about us?"

"But this man is an artist, madam. Society needs him healthy," whispered Duszek.

"I was an artist once, too," whispered the peasant woman. "But now I run a cattle farm. Let's drink to culture and art."

I took the cold traveling glass full of Scotch whiskey. "Let's drink to cattle breeding," I said resignedly.

"And what are you going to Kalisz for?" asked Kojran out of the blue.

"To a trial. My own."

Kojran whistled softly in surprise. "Who's taking you to court? The old colleagues you betrayed or the institutions you disappointed?"

"It's some man I don't know. He's taken it into his head that it's his life I've been describing in all my books."

"And have you been slandering him?"

"That's what he says."

"But weren't you really describing your own life?"

"Kojran, you know everything. Thank God that tomorrow you'll be flying off to America for good."

"Not everybody's leaving. There'll always be somebody here who knows something about you."

The door clattered. Someone was struggling with the plate glass covered with powdery snow. Finally, with a baleful screech, the door opened and a troop of people in sheepskin hats elbowed their way into the store. They were led by an energetic lady with a colossal behind, wearing tight slacks and a short sheepskin parka. The newcomers bunched together at the head of the line.

"What's this! We've been waiting since this morning!" cried the old woman who had taken advantage of the student's kindness earlier. Only now did it become apparent that she was not so very old and that one of the construction workers had been casting flirtatious glances at her for some time now.

The new arrivals said not a word, pressing against the

counter like deaf-mutes. Only the thick puffs of steam issuing from their mouths testified to their edginess.

"Hold on!" called Kojran. "Manager, what's the meaning of this? Special clients? They don't have time to stand
in line?"

The manager broke off a confidential conference with
the leader of the new customers and regarded Kojran
haughtily. "Your guess is correct. These are special clients.
These are guests from the Soviet Union."

"And they don't have to stand in line?" hollered
Grzesio and quickly changed places so they couldn't spot
who had shouted.

"No, they don't," answered the manager dispassion-
ately. "I told them that if the rings arrived before the store
closed, these people, that is, the tourists, could make their
purchases without having to stand in line."

Instead of abuse and protest, instead of despair and
anger, the crowd of locals fell into a sudden and unexpected depression. The store grew quiet. Someone's stomach gave an awful rumble. A faint whiff of the famous
perfume Moscow Nights drifted over from the newcomers.

"The first star's come out," said Iwona softly.

We went over to the window, blew on the glass, and
rubbed it with our gloves.

"Star? Where's the star?"

"There, over the roof, near the TV antenna." Iwona
pointed with a thin pink finger.

"That's a plane landing," said Kojran.

"A plane landing during a snowstorm? What are you
talking about?" objected Duszek. "It's an optical illusion.
We won't see any stars today. We'll break the Christmas
wafer in the dark."

I took a closer look at Iwona, who was standing in
profile not far from me. I had never liked her type, but still

I liked her. Dark, almost black hair, nearly an Afro, convex brown eyes, light-pink lips, and a complexion which was supposed to have been swarthy but had settled for a pallor warmed by a trace of color. I felt both tenderness and a timid glimmering of desire. I wanted to take her by her fragile wrist, though I knew I never would. Just as I would never touch any of the thousands of eighteen-year-old girls I see every day in the street. They move along a different shore. They swim in the same river I do but they are still close to the source. Fate had designated her for males several generations distant from me.

Iwona turned her face toward me. She looked at me and I lowered my eyes. This girl possessed the majesty of a mature woman. I remember such women from before the war, that long-forgotten era of regal women and manly men. This was no ordinary girl in jeans. My twenty-year-old equal was luxuriant with womanliness.

"Hello," I said.

"Hello." She smiled and my heart stopped for a moment.

"Where have you been?"

"You prefer blondes."

"I always liked them all. I never was prejudiced."

"How's your cat Ivan?"

"You know my cat?"

"I've read your book about him."

The blizzard was subsiding. The houses on the other side of the street were now visible, the bodies of hares powdered with fresh snow hung from balconies. A tall, thin woman was approaching from the direction of the rotary. I looked at her through the damp glass and felt there was something wrong. In her vigorous gait, in the way her head was tilted back, in her astonishing slenderness, I sensed some overwhelming, tragic abnormality. For a moment a piece of the window frame blocked her from view. I waited in suspense for her to reappear. Iwona, who had begun writing something with her finger on the cold glass, was waiting too. Finally she reappeared. She was walking down the middle of the sidewalk. People passed her, paying her no attention, but suddenly they began stopping in their tracks, amazed, turning, and following her with their eyes through the fine, still-dry snow. It was only then that I saw that this woman, or rather girl, was walking casually, wearing an ankle-length calico dressing gown patterned with large chrysanthemums; she was raising the hem of that dressing gown with two fingers like the hem of a ball gown, and from beneath that chrysanthemum-patterned dressing gown flashed a rose-colored silk nightgown. Suddenly I spotted her bare feet sunk in the snow as in the sand at a beach; then, shaken, I saw her fair head thrown back, her face young, girlish, but strained with madness, set in some ultimate decision, the face of a ghost or a corpse risen from the dead, a face you might dream of on an ominous, full-moon night.

The barefoot woman in the dressing gown passed the jewelry store. She looked up and ahead as if at distant Praga, as if into that vast space from which the icy east winds swoop down. Then she vanished behind the embrasure of the display window. All that remained were the tracks of her bare feet and the snowy landscape of a fading city on Christmas Eve.

"You know, I'm embarrassed by our conversation," I said.

"What embarrasses you about it?"

"Its banality. The banality of its unseemliness."

"Are you thinking of the difference in our ages?"

"I'm constantly thinking about the black wake of time behind me."

"I don't feel any difference."

"I don't feel any, either. But I know, and that's worse."

105

"What kind of miracle are you waiting for?"

"The miracle of understanding. People have been waiting for a miracle like that for thousands of years."

"Do you hope to be the first to understand?"

"Yes, I do, though it still may not happen. But lately that's what I've been living for, that's all that absorbs me. There are moments when it seems the process of understanding has begun, as if I'd caught hold of the first link, the first rosary bead, but a moment later that little flame dies out, blown out by biology, the daily grind, the world, and once again I begin the process preparatory to understanding, I begin concentrating all my spiritual powers and wait for that dazzling miracle which the few people who have died and been brought back to life by doctors have been able to remember. But they do not know how to formulate their impressions into a generalized axiom, an eschatological conclusion, into an ejaculatory act of new faith or new consciousness. That I could do, I've been prepared for years. I am waiting for that explosion every hour of the day and night, every hour, good or ill, every hour marked by the Milky Way, or else it's all an illusion."

"And what if I told you, what if I gave you a formula you could decipher and explain?"

"You work here till four o'clock and then later you'll go to your business classes at night school. Lots of pretty girls from good homes drop out of school and work in offices as messengers or as secretarial help in order to have the right to attend night school, receive diplomas, that receipt which gives them a chance of a modest start in life. Your mama bought you a warm, fashionable turtleneck sweater, Daddy set aside money for a trip to Bulgaria in case you pass your exams, and your grandma prays every night that you won't get yourself in any trouble."

Iwona smiled and with the palm of her hand erased the beginning of a hieroglyph or physics equation from the window. "I finished a regular high school, then I received my master's. My grandma doesn't pray that I don't get myself in trouble. I'm sorry, but I'm not that young."

The Soviet tourists were treating the men in line to Soviet luxury cigarettes. The weary customers shifted from foot to foot, sloshing in the mud covering the alabaster floor.

"What do you think, why was that girl walking barefoot in a dressing gown through a snowstorm on Christmas Eve?"

"She must have been going through something she couldn't get through."

"Nobody even dared stop her."

"We felt intimidated, too. A religious fear of the ultimate."

Kojran walked over, elegantly holding a Soviet filter cigarette between two fingers.

"You see, I didn't forget you," he said to me, casting a bloodshot glance over at Iwona. "And perhaps you smoke, too, miss?"

"Thanks, but I don't." Iwona went behind the counter and stroked the candle's edge so that the wax would not drip down it.

"You got her lined up?" asked Kojran.

"Doesn't look like it. I think I got off on the wrong foot."

"Your books are weak in that area, too. Sluggish, not real. More poison than passion. Do you really think about the war at moments like those or are you just torturing yourself with the difficulty of getting an erection?"

"I torture myself a little, but I'm not thinking about the war. If I'm thinking, it's about many things. Like when you're dying."

"Ugh, what a faker you are."

He lit my Soviet cigarette. In the flickering match

light I could see his hands, clean, yet at the same time a little dirty, the hands of a man who leaves his house at daybreak and returns late. On the palm of his hand near the base of his thumb a faded, blue homemade tattoo from his youth—HONOR AND FATHERLAND; it had grown with his hand, blurring on the skin.

"And when are you going to Kalisz?"

"Right after the holidays. I have two days' grace."

"Have you ever seen the man who's bringing you to court?"

"No, never. But I feel his presence constantly. Even now, at this very moment. I can talk with Iwona, you, Duszek, but part of me is always in contact with that man, who has besieged me with letters, with novellas which are supposed to be a philosophic reply to my philosophy, with threats via distant acquaintances. He assaults me with his aggressive presence, so encrusted with hatred, so insistent on its mysteriousness. He is strong because he lives solely with the idea of destroying me, not the destruction of some individual person, a sandy blond of average height who can prove his identity with ID number SJ 6311687; no, this destruction is the extermination of some phantom, some hostile abstraction, some evil meaning amid all the meaninglessness. He has renounced all life's temptations, perhaps even divorced his wife, eats only roots, drinks tap water, and lives with the preternatural desire of grinding me into dust and scattering that dust in the upper strata of the atmosphere. He and I will be joined by appalling bonds until one of us dies. The trial is the first halting place in our mutual Golgotha."

"You should thank God that's all the trouble you got."

"What could be worse than someone else's bioenergy bombarding you twenty-four hours a day, even in your sleep, even when you pass out."

The electric lights came on. The jewelry store again

became an elegant European boutique. The manager extinguished the candles, stifling the flaming wicks with saliva-moistened fingers. Once again the distant carol played by the street band could be heard.

"Let's get back in line," decided Kojran. "If nature gave you such talent, it wasn't for nihilism and slovenliness. Write something that will lift our spirits, goddamit."

"You're right. That would be good. But somehow or other I've gotten everything tangled up. All the obligations, duties, rights. I don't know how to begin."

We resumed our places in a black puddle which reflected the golden brilliance of the crystal chandelier. The old woman who had turned out not to be so old, and who was now being amused by the construction worker, was struggling with a net bag in which an enormous carp was thrashing, trying in vain to die.

"He says," said the student, still interpreting for the anarchist, "that there's something in Poland. Some sort of spirit. Some force of eternal unrest. He's seen Polish films, he knows about the Polish school."

"Many unprejudiced people become quite taken by our country," said the woman in the pelisse.

*

The fortunes and misfortunes of nations are often reminiscent of the fortunes and misfortunes of individuals, of ordinary people from the crowd, from everyday, ineffectual existence. There are nations with an ounce of luck which become dazzling successes, and there are nations which are unlucky, losers, wretched. There are nations which, at a certain moment, are dealt a good card; then their fate takes a sudden turn for the worse and impetuously they begin to squander all they own down to their last cent; and there are also those to which fate portions out a modest measure of useless luck every epoch. There are greedy, grasping nations which one day become slack and passive, but there are also frivolous, insouciant nations which suddenly learn how to think and see ahead. There are base, venal nations which history suddenly makes heroic and noble, and there are venerable, upright nations which, in an evil hour, take the road down to usury, blackmail, pandering.

History fascinates me. I follow the lives of nations and individuals. I flounder up and down, back and forth, through Polish history. At times I am subject to emotion, sublime exaltation, and sometimes I plunge to the depths of humiliation and despair. And then I reach for the curriculum vitae of our sister Russia. Russia always had luck. The tsars slaughtered their own people, established the stupidest and most ignorant laws, embroiled themselves in the riskiest of wars, set unreal political goals, and the foolish always became the wise, the reactionary the progressive, and defeat was changed to victory. Peter I, one of the greatest tsars, had lost the war with the Turks, was the prisoner of the Grand Vizier, and, in that most unfortunate of moments both for himself and his state, he struck upon the idea of an ordinary bribe, a vile baksheesh passed from hand to hand, a tip of the sort we might give a plumber or a janitor. The Grand Vizier accepts the bribe, sets Peter free, history immediately begins patting the Russian giant's head, luck changes at once, and Russia enters the next stage of political power. A common bribe, a stack of money decides the fate of a gigantic state—one of history's merry jokes.

Its entire social, economic, and civilizational structure should have led, pushed, and hurled the Russian state into the abyss of ruin and nonexistence. The ignorant, obscurantist despotism, the barbarity of the higher spheres, the people's poverty, the arbitrary, stupid, venal officials, the unbelievable indolence of the leaders, the most reactionary laws and customs, the savagery of human relations, all this, instead of inundating the state in disgraceful anarchy, instead of demolishing the structure of the state, instead of eradicating the Russian people from the European community, all this went into the laborious building of old Russia's power, her supremacy, her greatness among the nations of the old continent.

In Poland the nobility of educated monarchs, the energy of intelligent ministers, the goodwill of the citizenry, the homage to mankind's lofty ideas, in Poland all these positive, exemplary, copybook values were, quite unexpectedly, devalued. Out of the blue, they were prostituted and dragged the venerable corpse of the republic straight to the bottom like a millstone.

We're well aware of what happened and why. Our historiographers have taken precise soundings of the vertebral column of Polish history. They have brought to light all manner of defects, faults, and degeneration. We know that our "golden freedom" was our undoing. That fierce, mad adherence to the freedoms of the individual citizen, the autonomy and independence of the person. All our troubles stem from that unbridled freedom. Our entire Golgotha comes from that untimely eruption of individualism. All our uncertainty about the future comes from that inexplicable inclination to set an unhampered "I" in opposition to "us," "you," or "them."

Like a bad pupil, like a dunce in the corner, like street hooligans, we are used as an example by the wise and bearded historiographers of our exemplary neighbors, who, instead of submerging themselves in freedom, making a god and a religion of it, built strong, despotic states based on tyranny, the staunch superiority of the state over the confused individual, a cult of crushing individuals in the name of the genocidal goals of mighty Molochs. Our history envies our beheaded neighbors with their lawless states, the ultimate captivity of the thinking beings called by biologists, our fellow historians, *Homo sapiens.*

But to hell with that unfulfilled career of despots and tyrants. To hell with that unrealized role as the gendarme of Europe. To hell with that abortive summoning of defenseless individuals and entire helpless nations to the hangman.

What is it that we should be ashamed of? A fondness for freedom? Even though it was a foolish, mad, total, anarchistic, provincial freedom, the freedom which leads to ruin.

I know, I know. I know full well those ominous examples of our golden freedom which gave rise to our nation's entire chain of misfortunes and tragedies, I see the immensity of the evil born out of old-time, Sarmatian, noble, selfish, nihilistic, unthinking, lone-wolf, egotistical Polish freedom. But had we been a disciplined, ordered, antlike society of the Anglo-Saxon variety, would we have been spared by acquisitive despots, would our aggressive, totalitarian neighbors not have quartered our corpse? For nobility will always succumb to villainy, virtue fall at the feet of crime, freedom perish at the hands of the unfree. Though one may equally say that righteousness will conquer sin, good be victorious over evil, freedom triumph over slavery. But let us remember that the good is free like a cloud in the sky and that evil is swift as lightning.

*

A cleaning woman appeared from the back of the store, carrying a pail, broom, and black cloth. Indifferent to the elegance of the store, the configuration of the line, and our boots, she began scraping the mud and transferring it to the pail with the cloth. We discreetly made way for her,

112

wiping off our pants legs when she splashed us. No one
had the courage to point out to her just how impractical
and ridiculous her job was.

"Give a Pole freedom, he'll outdo everyone," said
Duszek and fell silent at once, taken aback by the sudden
hush with which the line received his maxim.

"They won't be bringing any more goods," said
Grzesio finally.

"It looks that way," seconded the peasant woman
redolent of Dior. "Is anybody cold?"

She pointed at her silver glasses lacquered a pis-
tachio green. Discreetly Kojran let his cigarette butt fall
into a clump of mud and ground it out with his elastic-
sided boot, an export reject.

"If the Soviets are waiting, the goods are bound to
arrive."

In fact, the Soviet tourists were making themselves
quite at home. Cramped into a well-disciplined group,
they were dozing on their feet or looking lazily about at
the rococo decorations on the walls and ceiling. One of
them, however, was staring at me. He smiled good-naturedly, and somehow it was a familiar smile. I knew that
face from somewhere, I remembered those gray, nearsighted eyes, the broad nose, and the narrow lips the color
of earthworms in spring. He laughed at me and beckoned
me with his fingers, somewhat coarsely, somewhat fa-
miliarly. I looked carefully to check whether he might be
looking at someone else. No, my comrades in line were
gaping at the plate-glass counter without a thought in their
heads. It was me the Russian wanted, me he was sending
smiles, me his heavy, work-wearied hand was beckoning.

As I started walking uncertainly over to him, he
rushed up to me. "Tadzka? Konwicki?" he asked. "Jadwiga's son?"

"And are you Kaziuk? Konstanty's son?"

"Well, sure. And look how we meet, by pure chance."

We embraced, kissing each other on the cheek by the mouth. He smelled of bootleg tobacco and sheepskin, and I, no doubt, of Green Water shaving lotion.

"Just look, at the end of life we run into each other," said Kaziuk in amazement and smiled heartily, trustfully, joyfully, the way people who are only superficially sincere smile here.

"And to think we've never met once, isn't that so? I only knew your sister Alina, I met her once during vacation."

"We only heard about each other. But I recognized you right away. Everybody always said we were like two peas in a pod."

"Hold it, didn't we have a grandmother in common?"

"Right, we did. And my father's sister married your uncle. And Aunt Malwina's first husband was your mother's godfather. Then Jadwiga, your mother, was my mother's sister's sister-in-law. Those two brothers who lived near Wormiany married your mother's sister's daughters . . ."

"Hold on, I'm not getting any of this. But I remember you from the stories I heard. Didn't you fall off the roof and kill a rooster?"

"That's right. Our lives are connected, you and I. We never figured out the connections, but we are related by blood."

"So we are related, then?"

"Of course. Two peas in a pod."

"Where are you living now, Kaziuk?"

"At home. Not far from Oszmiana. How about you?"

"Here, in Warsaw."

"A person can live here, too," allowed Kaziuk.

A sweaty, grayish curl fell from under his sheepskin cap onto his forehead. A scrap of cigarette paper damp with blood had been pasted to his chin. Kaziuk was obviously still in the habit of shaving with a straight razor. I looked at his gray overcoat with its Oszmiana-style cut of fifty years back. I had set off to war in a coat like that once. Set off to conquer the world.

"The edge of the Rudnicka woods goes right up to where you live."

"It might have once, but that's going back. There's no more Rudnicka woods."

"What are you talking about?"

"No more Rudnicka, no more Nalibocka woods, no more Ruska woods. People cut them down. It's real Europe back home now."

We'd run out of things to talk about. We looked smilingly at each other, but the smiles were forced, and our cheek muscles had started aching from that long, continuous smile. So, once again, we embraced. I noticed his Soviet "Victory" wristwatch, and if he had been observant, he would have noticed mine as well.

"They say your mama's not alive?"

"That's right. And your parents?"

"Not living either."

"I guess you work in a kolkhoz?"

"Yes. I'm foreman of the pig farm."

"What's the name of your kolkhoz?"

"Same as them all. Victory. You must be a director by now?"

"Not quite yet. But I'm doing all right."

"You bought a sheepskin like a shepherd wears," Kaziuk remarked with something between admiration and reprimand.

"That's the fashion here now."

"You need any money? Don't be bashful. I've got a pocketful."

"I've got plenty, too. Had you needed . . ."

"It's hard to give away what's yours. There's money, there's just no life."

Kaziuk laughed at his own joke and punched the nape of my neck with his heavy hand. "Don't be scared. I love making jokes. I can do what I want because I'm a hero of socialist labor."

"Oh, you've risen pretty high, then. At least there's one out of the whole family."

"It happens. You want to see?" And without waiting for my answer, he unbuttoned his coat, revealing a gold star beside the lapel of his jacket.

For a long while neither of us said anything. Outside, a snowplow-tram was spinning in the snowdrifts. Both lines, the Soviet and the Polish, were observing us, but not openly, as we stood in the middle of the jewelry store, already tired of this unexpected meeting.

"Do you have children?" asked Kaziuk.

"I do. Two daughters. And you?"

"Me too. Two sons. The younger's in school, the older one's in the army already. Serving in the Caucasus."

"Do you ever get scared at night when you're back home, Kaziuk? I return there often. When I'm sick or depressed, sometimes in my dreams. I cross the border illegally in my cap of invisibility and homesickness. I walk the footpaths of my childhood, I swim in the rivers of my youth, I peek into the huts where I first gained my maturity."

"Watch out that the border guards don't grab you, Tadzka, or you'll wake up in prison." Kaziuk laughed. "Maybe you shouldn't have left Wilno?"

"What would my life be like now?"

"Like mine. We have a large kolkhoz. You couldn't see it all in three days. Room for everybody."

"Are you satisfied with your life?"

"I never think about it. It could be worse. How about you?"

"I'm constantly thinking about my life and I can't come up with anything."

"Man was created to work. I stay over by Oszmiana and look after our land, our forests, our prayers. That's all I know. The rest is bunk."

"You're a positive hero."

"What does that mean?"

I repeated it in Russian.

"We've got plenty of heroes." Kaziuk laughed.

Again I felt cold, and breathing was hard. No sudden pain pierced me, my hands weren't trembling, my head wasn't swimming, but I felt that I had slowly, with a sense of sadness, begun to die. I regarded myself with benevolent amazement and saw a horrible, gloomy darkness arising within me, black velvet lined with an unhurried dread. I did not feel any overwhelming weakness, but I wanted to lie down on the ground—it had to be cold ground—and press my cheek against the damp cold. I heard a muffled roar, everything began gradually receding as if seen through the wrong end of opera glasses. I wanted to make my hand reach out for a chair behind me, I wanted to say something amusing in farewell, and I wanted not to want.

On the horizon, the dawn of a new era. Mankind was slowly fusing into one new nation, Earthlings. The ease of transportation, of communicating information, thought, custom, and culture had reduced the once enormous universe of the world. The earth's sphere had become a husk on which we still are stricken by the fear of our unknown future.

Some sort of biological community is arising, the germ of a universal language is being forged which, at the beginning, may be a language of images, of posterlike hiero-glyphics designed by literature-hating professors. Politics and economics are uniting in ever-broadening areas. Contemporary art is becoming more universal, in many places state borders have become obliterated, more and more people of varying races and nations are intermarrying. Tomorrow we shall all be one great brotherly nation.

But today, as if foreseeing its own ruin, the sense of nation, tribe, region, is running riot, exploding, setting catastrophic reactions in motion. The smallest national groups, the quietest little islands, the most modest inheritors of long-extinct cultures are demanding freedom everywhere. Thus we see the old moldering bourgeois democracies sullenly capitulating before archipelagos of coral reef, ambitious countries, debauched human herds.

Freedom has suddenly become one of the most important resources of our already slightly exhausted earth. The exploitation of freedom is out in front in the statistics on the exploitation of the globe's resources. So, the day has come when freedom has become the number-one need. The freedom of nations, corporations, the freedom of the common, anonymous person who struggles with a tough life, a bad wife, and his own complete lack of ability. Universal democratization will render all the riches of the world to all people. Freedom included.

And, after all, we Poles were always ardent champions of freedom. We labored much in the risky process of discovering and spreading that divine vitamin. The nineteenth century was the era of our greatness and our downfall. For a century and a quarter or thereabouts, we howled like wolves about freedom, but you stopped up your ears. For a hundred years we Poles ran around the world bearing arms, providing cover for those in battle, and you denounced us as police agents.

It is true that, in brief moments of high-mindedness,

you held us up as symbols of freedom, but the next day you expelled us from your well-fed countries, which hold the freedom of the written and the spoken word in such esteem. Rarely did you kiss our martyred brows; more often you spat upon, scoffed at, and denigrated our struggle with stronger forces, a struggle which had nothing to do with highjacking planes full of innocent people, which knew nothing of kidnappings or murdering women and children.

Now freedom is passed out like bread. At the great bazaar of the United Nations everyone who wants freedom is portioned out a share. The colored and the colorless, the straight and the lame, the foolish and the wise, all bearing their handfuls, sackfuls, containerfuls of freedom from Manhattan. So, goddamit, why not give us a whiff of freedom, too?

*

I woke up in heaven. I was in the very center of a soft warmth, in the very heart of the benign. I felt so light, so light, as if the weight of my body had been taken from me. I heard a music serene and majestic composed in heaven by Haydn for the archangels' choirs. A pale, rose-colored light suffused the fragrant air, light from paradise, though it could have reminded someone of the color of the antechambers to hell. Above me hung a three-dimensional image of an angel familiar to all from old Mediterranean paintings. I saw Afro-like dark hair, I saw sweet convex eyes, I saw slightly puffed lips and the loveliness of a neck covered by pale yet at the same time burning skin.

"Do you want to live?"

"Part of me does, Iwona."

"Don't call me Iwona. If you prefer, I can be Basia."

"All right, Iwona. You can be Basia. But why Basia?"

"Doesn't matter, Basia sounds better. It brings back memories. So, do you want to live?"

"Not all that much. I've lived long enough."

"Don't exaggerate. I don't see a single gray hair on your head."

"That's true, I'm a bit ahead of my hair. But if it's a question of what you go through, I've been through it all. I have no curiosity left, my curiosity's exhausted, or actually, it was never satisfied and now nothing will satisfy it."

"What else would you like to know?"

"One ultimate question keeps forcing itself on me, a question terribly banal, tiresome, and irritating because it's continually harassing every person throughout his existence, a question indecent in its impotence, a shameful question because it has no answer, the sort of question ambitious people never ask. I'm quietly waiting for a miracle. I'm constantly waiting for an answer. I delude myself that one night someone close to me who has died—my father, my mother, a friend, a certain girl who committed suicide for no reason—will come to me, a ghost will give me the answer I've been waiting for all these years and will probably never receive."

"You already told me about that question and I offered to give you a formula to decipher on those long winter nights."

"Let's say you are an exotic consciousness from an exotic galaxy in our Milky Way or from a million other exotic Milky Ways, that you've clothed that alien consciousness of yours, or rather that superior supraconsciousness, in the standard earthling garb of a human body and have chosen that clothing of flesh with some taste and wear it casually, nonchalantly, heedlessly, as if it were a scrap of cosmic wind or a handful of seaweed from the canyons of the universe."

"All right, let's say I am a soul from another dimension who has incarnated herself, rather handsomely, to judge from your words. You shouldn't have any objections, I prefer being a soul to a consciousness."

"That incarnation was pretty risky. Had providence gone a shade further, you would have lost me as a client."

"Praised be destiny for its foresight. Will you also agree that I have selected you from among a couple of hundred thousand people and am waiting for the moment when your sun enters the sign of Capricorn, that is, when your earth tilts the final millimeter toward death and then begins its return to life, when you, in that motionless second, begin to long for your unknown future and your mysterious past."

"I agree. But it's getting a bit too much already. I always had a weakness for slightly mysterious women. But only slightly mysterious."

I could not see the walls or the ceiling. There was a rose-colored darkness everywhere. And a music full of the voices of bells or triangles. She smelled like the wild herbs of the earth.

I reached out for her with my strangely light hands. She bent toward me. I could feel her cold breath on my cheeks. There was consent in her eyes, or rather curiosity about my heightened sense of feeling. So I raised my light hand a bit; now our faces were so close that the warmth of her mouth touched my lips.

"Well and so?" I said.

"So, nothing," she answered.

"Let's see if angels have mouths."

We kissed, looking into each other's eyes. Something was happening within the pupils of her eyes, as if shuttered blinds were closing, then rising. As if fear, pain, or some memory had flashed past. Her lips tasted like trampled spring grass, no, it was the fleeting sweetness of a spring birch or young maple sap I recognized. Suddenly I felt a mounting roar inside myself, the roar of spring, and I saw that I wasn't so old, and that overwhelming trembling I remembered from years past was awakening in me again. I pushed back her turtleneck sweater and touched the slender span of ribs covered by warm, pulsing skin. She took off her camisole like any mortal. I embraced her breasts, real breasts, full of life, breasts from erotic dreams, the sort of breasts borne by women in my youth. Her breasts were crowned with lovely nipples, honeyed craters of dazzling mystery. Such breasts as you can find but once in your life, and, God willing, not too late. The nipples did not taste like grass or sap but of the sun, July heat, the sultry hour before nightfall.

"You had a heart attack," she murmured.

"Let's see if angels have earthly breasts."

"Aren't you afraid of death?"

"It's no time to be thinking about nonsense like that."

The trembling turned into convulsions of the sort which had swept over me even back in my Wilno days when I was still learning the alphabet of desire. I struggled with the angelic garments protecting her and me from sin. I peeled them from her decorously and then she was with me, hot, breathless, as real as in a dream or nostalgia. Without quite realizing it, I too was now naked, hot, and even young, perhaps. Haydn or some other celestial musician broke into a song. Her legs were the wings of a white swallow, wings spread for flight.

"Let's find out if angels are girls."

"No, no, your heart's beating awfully fast."

"It's beating its way to yours."

We were overcome by darkness, the red night of closed eyes. Brief darkenings covered our pounding arteries, our hoarse incantations, her, or my inhuman cry piercing Haydn's soaring song. We listened to that cry for a long time as it began to quiet our infinite moment of overwhelming happiness or the delight which seems to be happiness. Cold sweat trickled down my back like drops of spring rain.

"Move, old man," murmured Basia.

She kicked off the rest of our clothes with her legs and then lay shamelessly naked on her back, her arms flung out to the side, the palm of her hand having come to rest on the nape of my neck. She was breathing greedily, with gusto. I watched the gentle rise of her breasts with their taut, fully contracted nipples. Beneath her white skin light-blue veins were pulsing, the real earthly conduits of her circulatory system. A rosy mist of sweat gleamed on her neck. But that rose color kept shifting, for, swinging above us, was a lamp whose bare bulb had been carelessly covered with the red cover of some illustrated magazine. The lamp had been sent swaying by our frenzy and was now slowly abating.

"Don't call me an old man. That's all I ever call myself."

"But you are an old man. Look at the folds on your belly."

"That's because I'm lying relaxed. You should see me running on the field."

Basia, the former angel, yawned, her mouth wide open. I caught a glimpse of the bottom teeth, a filling in one molar. She was just a woman, a tall, good-looking young woman. I lay my hand on her warm stomach and she did not recoil from this intimate gesture. She was looking up at the magazine doubling as a lampshade. The light from the bulb shone through the letters of the intriguing title.

"Go to a doctor like I told you," she said lazily.

"Was there something wrong?"

She turned to me and kissed my temple casually.

"As far as that goes, everything was fine. But still, you passed out in the store."

"I drank too much."

"A man your age has to take care of his heart."

"Are you starting in on my age again?"

"Don't take offense, I like older men."

"Damnit, there's something weird about becoming an old man day by day."

"How old are you?"

"What do you care?"

Basia smiled, pushing a lock of hair from her pale forehead. "I've gotten to like teasing you."

Only then did I realize why I felt so warm. There was an electric heater beside the stained settee on which we were lying, and its red-hot coils were pointed directly at us. Haydn had already concluded his performance. The weather report came on. Blizzards, frosts, sudden thaws, constant rain. Somewhere a bay had frozen, somewhere crocuses were in bloom. A flood in one place, people dying of thirst in another.

"Listen, old man, why do you bother with those ultimate questions of yours; why are you waiting for a miracle when you really can't even rise an inch off the sidewalk? After all, it's really the earth that concerns you, not heaven. Before your heart attack you were always furious about life's petty details."

"How do you know me so well?"

"Let's say, from school."

"I'm curious what kind of school that is. Because they don't read me in regular schools."

"You tear yourself in two, holding on to heaven with one hand and earth with the other."

"I probably do. The way I vegetate torments me, and what bothers me even more is the fate of those strange, stupid, unfortunate people with whom I live beside a fairly large river poisoned by wastes from a bungled industrial development."

"Slow down, you're getting mixed up."

"You're right. In two places at once. I'm a foreigner and I've taken my adopted country too much to heart."

"What makes you a foreigner?"

"What makes you one?"

"I'm Basia, in my fourth year of business school. I'm doing my practical in a jewelry store where I was seduced by an elderly customer. It's a good thing I'm over eighteen, otherwise you'd be in big trouble."

On a small crooked table covered with a paper tablecloth, the radio was blinking its old-fashioned green cat's eye. A large symphony orchestra was playing a festive Polish Christmas carol. In apartment caves beneath mountains of snow, people were breaking the traditional Christmas wafer.

"Where am I, Basia in the fourth year of business school?"

"In my room at boarding school. Or in the employees' room in the back of a jewelry store. As you prefer."

"I'd rather it was a mountain pass on a summer day."

"Do you like the mountains?"

"I hate the mountains. Spoil the view."

"You fell back all of a sudden and that friend of yours wouldn't let anyone else help you. But he was just faking it—he would have beaten you up happily."

"Who? Kojran?"

"The one who's flying to America tomorrow. To the world after this one."

"Kojran. He's right. I do owe him my life."

"Do you always talk like this with women?"

"I have less and less to do with women all the time. And more to do with girlfriends."

125

"Maybe we can become friends, too? You could come by the shop at seven when I get off. In the winter we could go to the movies; then afterward we could hug and kiss by my gate. In the summer you could take me down beside the Vistula, to the willow woods where the birds sing. You'll tell your friends confidentially that you've got a little brunette who's crazy over you even though she's thirty years younger than you are. I'll save scarce jewelry for you. We'll go on like that for a few years until your poor health stops us or I resign myself to getting married."

"Why are you telling me all this?"

"Because I'd marry you. I've had my eye on you for a long time. You're delicate, sensitive, completely different. Women love men like that."

"I can't, child. I had a Roman Catholic wedding, and you know what that means."

"Unfortunately I do. A marriage only God can dissolve."

"That leaves us the movies and the beach by the Vistula. If, of course, you'd want that."

"I'll think that proposition over, though it doesn't hold much of a future."

"Aren't you cold?"

"Are you embarrassed to see me naked?"

"No, happy. I'm ashamed because my indecent lust is returning."

There was a calendar on the mottled wall. Someone had crossed out all the days of Christmas ahead of time. Time stood still waiting for people to catch up. If they lived that long.

Basia was larger naked than when clothed. Her large, relaxed nipples stared up at the smoke-darkened ceiling. I kissed the one closest to me and immediately it turned sweet as honey. Basia pretended not to see but held her breath. I slid my fingers along her pulsing belly until I met

126

the dry weeds of her curly hair. Basia felt everything, looking somewhere off to one side, probably at the green cat's eye of the radio, which was dripping with sentimental Christmas carols.

"Leave me alone, there's no need to," whispered Basia, though she spread her legs and raised her knees.

I caressed her in the proper places, seeing all of her in front of me, all the mysteries which had been swathed in the reddish light of the lamp and had now lost their mystery in the minutes or hours we'd been lying there.

"Don't strain yourself, old man," she whispered, squeezing my hand between her thighs and releasing it at once.

"I'll give you old man."

I slid up lazily onto her body magnified by its nakedness, found the path, and she obligingly assisted me, sighing when I was in deeply.

"Maybe we should put it off till tomorrow," I murmured in her ear.

"Never mind, let's get on with it," she said in an attempt at a dispassionate reply.

She was sincere, or becoming more sincere, while I, devious as a fox, faker from way back that I am, joined in her rapture, feigning ecstasy, and when she suddenly grew taut and then faded as if actually dying, I carefully and stealthily began all over from the beginning.

Her lips barely moving, she pronounced her verdict: "You deceived me."

"I don't know. I don't know what I'm doing."

Her lips spread slightly apart in an inward smile. Then they slowly returned to that shape which signifies a sleepy, tender kiss. Finally she closed her eyes. It was then that the strange, uncontrollable force seized me. I wanted to pretend, to deceive, to trick her out, but I could not, I couldn't stop, couldn't delay. And so, together, in harmony, we were clasped by that pain which is the gift of God or nature, and clinging to each other, we flew headlong toward the blinding red flare of light.

"And so?" I asked, gulping the burning, ferrous air.

She snuggled up against me and hugged me. Gasping for breath, I couldn't see anything. She kissed my aging lips and my nearsighted eyes and whispered bashfully, "It was all right. Though I've probably overstepped my role as an employee."

"I tried. But too late."

"It's never too late, as people say on all sorts of occasions when it is too late."

"Are you taking a course in the propaedeutics of philosophy at school?"

"And what is it that bothers you, old man, the riddle of existence or the misfortunes of those closest to you, those who speak the same language you do?"

"Sometimes one, sometimes the other. I see that now. I'll have to start keeping accounts, my little jewelry-store employee, to check just how much of my sinful life I've wasted."

"It wasn't so long ago you were committing adultery."

"That may be the one thing the good Lord will forgive me. If He's taken any note of this old man's ambitions, evaluated the riskiness of his endeavors, He'll surely forgive me."

"Did you ever suspect that I wanted to kill you? To kill you with your own last spasm of desire?"

"Why would you want to kill me?"

"Maybe it'd be better if you perished here and now."

"I see you know what awaits me. I'd look you in the eye but I don't have the strength."

Once again she kissed me with a certain disturbing care.

"Why don't you say something?" I asked.

"Give me a cigarette. Everything turned out different."

"What should have happened?"

"What do you want from me? I just remembered that I have a lot of work for tomorrow."

"But you didn't go to school today."

"I didn't?" said Basia in surprise. "You're right, I didn't. And tomorrow's a holiday."

"So can we make a date for after the holidays?"

"Is it worth it?"

"I don't know. Right now I've got too many scruples. But maybe I'd start missing you."

"You poor old man."

"Not so bad as all that. Sometimes I forget myself. Or maybe I'd like to be like everyone else. All in all, the biggest loss is mine."

"You know what, maybe I'll give you a call, all right?"

A meager streak of smoke was issuing from the magazine cover which served as a lampshade. The bulb was scorching the paper.

"All right."

"No. You'll just wait by the phone and that'll be torture for you."

"Yes, it would, a little. I'm not even going to ask how you know me so well."

"In that case, I'll come see you. Or maybe I won't, either.

"All right. You come see me. Or maybe you won't. Maybe I'll come see you, or maybe not."

"And how would you know where to find me?"

"In the jewelry store, or could be at school, or maybe on the first planet of the Milky Way."

"All right, Konwa. Is that what people call you?"

"They did when I was young, several epochs ago, no, rather several eras decisive in human evolution ago."

"Come on, give me a light, then."

I started looking for my jacket, which I found stuffed inside my sheepskin coat. I groped for the pockets. A tell-tale rustling sound in one of them. Must be the money. I half pulled out a letter in a torn envelope stamped lavishly by our postal service and our meticulous customs service. That colorful envelope contained a letter from Seweryn P., a childhood friend. The last time we'd seen each other was in front of my house in the Wilno Colony, at dawn, the sixth of June 1944. Both of us had French carbines and no ammunition, and we were both running to attack a German Panzer tank which had been detained at our little train station by the Wilno Uprising—we, too, had an uprising toward the end of the war, though few remember it, and even I recall it with increasing infrequency. I'd been walking around with Seweryn's letter, Sewka's letter, for several weeks, unable to part with it. I keep feeling his fading pulse inside myself. I keep hearing his stinging chants like obscure pangs of conscience.

"What happened?" asked Basia anxiously. "Is your heart bothering you?"

"It'll always be bothering me now."

*

Dear Friend and Friend of my youth,

I expect my letter to reach you and only that irrational hope justifies the effort made by the many noble people who helped forward it on its way. I don't know your address and so I have put only your name and country on the envelope. Writing that word "Poland" made me aware of many complicated and upsetting sentiments and presentiments.

I know that you're alive, that the war did not wipe you from the face of our weary earth, since in the Polish press (Poland is now my stepmother land), in that squalid press, I read an abusive review of a film of yours that had been in some minor festival.

I am currently in the hospital, a large overcrowded building full of pain, suffering, and misfortune. But for the first time in many years all these misfortunes are humanizing me, constructing invisible walls of safe asylum around me, separating me from the inhuman circumstances in which my adopted fellow citizens must live. The system and its practices, all the loathsome brutality of human violence, has to stop at the doorway of this dismal building, this melancholy combination of a laboratory and a funeral chapel. My asylum is ruled by old age, an apolitical fate; common, horrible death paces the stone corridors of my asylum at night, and from this place, the far-distant shore, the beginning of an ominous infinity can be seen.

The reason I find myself here is not an elevated one. To wit, I am suffering from a vulgar asthenia of the anus but, with a certain amazement, I have discovered that my illness is treated with the same seriousness as a heart attack or an old gunshot wound. Hence, one deduces that no matter what brings a man to this sanatorium he can leave only by the exit which leads to the mortuary.

The head of the ward, who treats me with a certain degree of care, is a famous proctologist and, even more important, a decent, non-Party type. And for that reason he would never have been able to hold such a responsible position, and would never have been able to give me any help in sending this letter on its way, had it not been for the fact that a certain influential government minister was also suffering from the same illness as mine. His is a real case, though, a chronic case which apparently even threatens the life of that unknown dignitary. Consequently, my ward head has recently become an unofficial, even secret personal physician to the statesman. For that reason, from time to time, he is part of the minister's entourage when he travels outside the country, this nicely disguised prison. These observations inclined me to take a risk, the tempting risk of sending a note from prison out to the distant, free world. What would I choose if not old, liberal Europe, if not my mad homeland, if not you, with whom I learned to smoke my first cigarette, you and I who fell in love with the same girl, you and I who tried to fight for the very freedom that all the unfree people in the world dream of.

Drawn into an ambush of moral obligations, my non-Party physician decided, not without some fear and dismay, to bring my letter out to the first free country and to toss it into a mailbox on the sly. So, if they don't strip him at the airport, if they don't ferret out this tangled manuscript, you will be receiving a letter from the other world; but the other world here on earth, which, in my opinion, is just an ordinary hell that barely even works right.

I will, however, begin at the beginning. When the war was over I made my way to the West (Western Europe, of course). I tried a number of different possibilities, but none of them led anywhere. And so, I set off to seek my fortune on another continent, as a great many other castaways had done before me. I ended up in a rather sympathetic country whose history had been stormy and dramatic, a country which had been free for a few decades, was not too well off but not too poor either, and was inhabited by frivolous, slightly romantic people gifted with a sense of humor. As you see, all this could remind me a little of my lost homeland.

I had barely gotten my bearings when a shocking surprise occurred. Influenced by its omnipotent neighbor to the north, a change of government took place. A junta backed by that neighbor seized power and, supplied with coffers, or rather with supply trains, set with dead seriousness about the business of governing. They proclaimed a

very definite obligatory ideology and an unbelievably rad-
ical social program. Briefly stated, they had no regard for
the life already there and began building an entirely new
existence. There was only one force, a single monopolistic
political party which was run by the appointed leader. At
first he was anonymous and completely unpopular, but, in
the course of time, he slowly grew sanctified and was
gradually transfigured by hysterical propaganda into a
universal intelligence or, more simply put, a God. Naturally you know implanting this political religion cost a few
hundred thousand human lives. By the way, I should add
that, for a time, I too was under the spell of this aggressive
religion, though to you, a citizen of old, gentle Europe, this
will seem bizarre and beyond comprehension.

How can I describe my life to you, my fate from
which there is no turning back? Perhaps it will be best for
me to tell you that I have no life and no fate. My life is a
constant complaint in some strange, tasteless, colorless
suspension, or rather, one with an empty, unfermented
taste which turns into bitterness and gray hopelessness.
My fate is black fly specks on pages of falsified statistics.
The very essence of my existence is that, from morning to
night and even in my sleep, I do not feel like living, my
life makes me puke, I dream about death, but a death of
my own; a personal death, at one's own responsibility,
turns out to be difficult to accomplish, most likely because
it conflicts with the state's version of death, the ideological,
mass death offered to us every day by the regime.

Our Party, which has a long and fine-sounding name,
even lovelier in an exotic tongue, reminds me of a gigantic
vacuum cleaner which sucks in everything within the
compass of this ill-fated country's borders. It could also be
likened to a cancer which greedily burns its way through
every inch of tissue, every cell of the body politic, an in-
furiated cancer, a cancer in total overdrive, a cancer with a

cosmic erection. Perhaps there has occurred, or is now occurring, in Europe, a degeneration in the functioning of
states and in their dealings with one another, but there is
no way you can imagine the nightmare that has befallen
us.

We are duty-bound to official love for our northern
neighbor and to love for our own country. But that love of
country, that patriotism of ours, is a hitherto-unknown
value, a new discovery in the region of high governmental
sentiment. The main component of our patriotism is a
hysterical, unbridled, and slightly perverted love for our
neighbor to the north, but only as if it were a supplement,
a sumptuous dressing to top off one's love of country.
Thus, in the final analysis, both types of official love fully
resemble each other, since, in both, the cornerstone, the
opaline cornerstone, turns out to be a whorish lust for our
ruthless neighbor.

Late summer blazes outside my window. Still succulent, still green, still cheerful, but already in its precipitate
and melancholy decline. For the last few days an old man
has lain dying in one of the rows of extra beds out in the
corridor. Surrounded by IVs he hums or yelps protest
songs of his own. A while back he shat in bed and smeared
the wall and the bed, state property, with his excrement.
Now he lies in derisive apathy, listening to the complaints
of the orderlies who have to clean and change him. Soon
he'll start tearing the needles from his arms and demolishing those modest contrivances which are supposed to restore him to life. Only now, at the end of his road, has he
risen in revolt against the slavery imposed on men by other
men.

Yes, our ideology is like a religion. In fact, it is a
continuation of religion, for in this ill-fated land people's
souls have been ruled for ages by a depraved religion and
a venal church. Religion in the service of the state, religion

directed by the head of state. And the essence of that religion has always been form, a hyperbolized, mythologized, absolutized form. And the most important element in that form was the word. But the word never became flesh. The word lived its own superior life. A magical, abstract life. The word ignored reality, human intelligence, the moral instincts. The word became a bloody tyrant, the word became a cruel superstition, a merciless god.

Our all-envying Party killed that compromised religion. From its sacred, sinful corpse it did, however, remove the vestment of form and the amulet of the word. Now form and the word serve the Party. Now the Party bows down to the word, its own servant. But that servant, the word, now holds the Party captive, though the Party had intended to make the word into an obedient fetish. Now the Party submits its existence, the fate of the state, and the wheeling of stars and galaxies to the word.

We all live in savage fear of the word. The word terrifies the Party and the ministries, the word causes dread in generals and censors, words frighten when heard in bugging devices or in the inadequately controlled dreams of citizens. And worst of all is the written word, the word fixed in orthographic or phonetic signs on paper, strips of celluloid, or marble. And that is why I trace these lines with such panic in this misty lake of pain and misfortune, this sanctuary of momentary freedom before my annihilation.

As you probably remember, I was the best at drawing when we were in high school. You certainly also must remember that I used to send my drawings in to all sorts of contests for youth and that my work would be sent back with outraged letters threatening to inform the principal about my attempted fraud, for the jurors considered my drawings those of a mature artist and assumed that I had stolen them or tricked them out of someone to enter them under my own name and win the prize. So you remember, if in general you care to remember your childhood, you remember my artistic abilities, which I kept with me until I reached this country. I wanted to make some use of them. But the Party got hold of my talent. It seized my hand and closed it in its pincers and began leading it across the paper, so that my every stroke sang the praises of the Party, so that every dot was a loving sigh to the Party, and every flourish expressed gratitude to the Party. For we are all marked by original sin, some terrible unclear sin against the Party. The Party is angered, the Party has taken it ill, it is hard for the Party to keep its patience. But we should be humble, beseech its mercy on our knees; lying flat on our faces, we are obliged to thank the Party every hour, thank it that we are alive, eating, going to factories, moving our bowels, traveling by train, reading Party newspapers; thank it for being bored in the evening, for the sun shining, for autumn coming, for the atmosphere surrounding the globe. The expression of gratitude is the essence of our lives. We were born to be able to express gratitude to the Party.

To protect myself against the insolent presence of the Party, I decided to abandon graphic art for history. History is the past, the forgotten rubbish pile in which the clochards of totalitarian societies can rummage about. But no chance of that, my fortunate friend, for even there in that would-be refuge the festering, rapacious Party was waiting for me, ransacking poor history like a dung hill. It was no longer history; now it was a heap of equally facile lies accompanied by the strong smell of educational content. I had jumped from the frying pan into the fire. And there was no longer any place to run. I had changed my entire life so that it was the life of dead people, dead societies, dead ideas.

In Poland winter is now slowly coming to an end. The

snows are melting, the west wind brings the distant aroma of the new. I tried to recall our Polish days of early spring, full of expectation, foreboding, and hope. When inwardly I say that one short word "Poland," a wistful exaltation arises in me, something clear, free, soothing; Poland, homeland of freedom; Poland, lair of tolerance; Poland, that great garden of rampant individualism. Where people greet each other with a smile, where a policeman lifts a rose instead of a club, where the air is made of oxygen and truth. Poland the great white eagle in the center of Europe.

Our regime was on its last legs right from the start. It was rotting, gurgling, disintegrating, moldering, rusting, choking, dying, and yet at the same time standing firmly on its feet, enduring due to the immense power of inertia, withstanding all storms, entrenched in bedrock by the weight of its own sins. What chemical ingredient perpetuates this rot? What drives this machine, which is out of control and half worn out? Whose will protects this satanic vessel from being struck by divine lightning?

The magical proximity of the northern colossus is what supports our agonized movements. That great cobalt bomb of imperial aspirations bombards us day and night, every hour, every moment, with trillions of atoms of corruption, treachery, venality, bribery, nihilism, provocation, hatred, moral indifference, and total capitulation. We ourselves support the regime and its agonized movements. Our peculiar desire to dominate those nearest us oils the notched gears, runs the drive belt, stokes the fire. Our regime has given the stupid a chance to rule the wise, permitted villains to humiliate the honest, commanded the strong to torture the weak.

Power. Delight in power. The magic of power. The opium of power. To have power over an individual and a social group. To have power over objects and the spirit of a stranger. To have power over history and futurology. To subdue one's brother and go into ecstasies over one's own omnipotence. At every rung of the ladder—Party cell, metallurgical combine, television station, or the highest Party congress. To suit one's whims, animosities, and complexes, to be able to mobilize the apparatus of the state, the executive power of the Party, the editorial boards of newspapers, the police, the army. Day by day sculpting one's own monument, every instant building a pyramid of unbridled pride, defying if only once the laws of nature and the laws of God. Will this apotheosis of petty tyranny endure a single day after your death? Perhaps it will. Perhaps for the first time in human history it will endure and rouse the admiration and envy of the species for all time.

The cancer of power. Power run amok. The abyss of power. An abyss engulfing millions of consciences and millions of souls.

The dense, early spring sun is warming a light-blue, slogan-covered banner spread out along one wall of the hospital. The slogan calls the patients to battle. But at this time of afternoon the patients are loafing shamelessly. They are sleeping unkempt, semi-feverish, deprived of care; forgetful of eavesdroppers and informers, they talk to themselves in anti-government dreams, groan demoralizingly, curse blasphemously. The Party seems to have capitulated, seems to have left them in peace, but still somewhere out there it is racking its hydra head thinking how to make the most ideological mileage out of people at death's door.

In a short while I'll go out to the corridor and then to the lounge crowned with dozens of luminous signs on the doorway leading to the surgical ward. This is our triumphal arch, our sanctuary. There providence draws its first lots. But today workers are on the move. Special workers, police workers. They have already removed the superfluous patients from the hall and are painting the walls, screwing in new bulbs, and searching for hidden mines and time bombs with special devices. For tomorrow a member of the Party directorate will be brought here; a most important personage, though anonymous, for he is known only by the name mentioned scores of times each day in the newspapers and by the voice heard stammering on radio and television. It is precisely that stammering which is to be eliminated in this hospital. Tomorrow, our neurosurgeon—also a high-ranking Party member—tomorrow, with trembling hands, he will open the thorax of his colleague from the directorate and plunge in a lancet checked out by security agents, a lancet which will perhaps sever the proper nerve and enable the leader to express himself correctly at conferences and meetings. This will happen tomorrow, the mystery will be revealed tomorrow, but today there is a flurry of civilians and police, a flurry like that before a première or state holiday. And I am taking a sacrilegious part in this flurry; I am known here as a mildly ill patient, someone who likes to help other patients and hospital personnel, and so I will shuffle along the stone floor already inspected by the mine detectors, touch the walls sticky with fresh paint, walls in which wires for bugging devices have been installed, and breathe air swirling with molecules of political suspicion.

My final encouragement in this ravine of despair before death, my final gleam of sudden hope, my final breath of life-giving oxygen is the memory of my country, that country which, my dear friend, I have lost forever.

O Poland, mother to all the wronged and humbled, fare thee well.

O Intercessor, for the captive and the lost, fare thee well.

O Protectress of all those whose eyes and tongues have been torn out, fare thee well.

O Widow of those murdered at the crossroads of the

world, O Widow of ghosts who will never waken the conscience of the world, fare thee well.

I am a slave. I have been delivered unto a modern
slavery. Slavery in the era of ribonucleic acid, computers,
and satellites. Ancient slaves in the epoch of undisguised
slavery had a good life. They are to be envied. What phe-
nomenal careers! What a wonderful start in life! What a
comfortable existence at someone else's expense! Our
school textbooks tried to intimidate us with their fate,
those unlucky slaves who could win the confidence of their
masters, win their friendship, even their love, and receive
property from them, their daughter's hand, or real freedom. Why didn't providence make me a slave of a Roman
consul, why was I fated to vegetate as a slave of the state,
the Party, and idiotic social doctrines?

I am a slave. I am a slave deprived of his own individual face. I am the slave of a collective slavery. My
anonymous master does not know me. He will never reward me, show me his love, or grant me my freedom. I am
a slave hidden in the horrifying and not always truthful
numbers of the state's statistics.

I am allowed to work, eat moderately, and take brief
periods of rest to restore my strength for more work; in the
statistics and in the mentality of my unknown masters it is
only my physical ability to work that counts, for it serves
to build the pyramid of our great modern arrogance. My
work-ox ability is measured on a daily basis, translated
into numbers and percentages, and announced in the newspapers, on television, in reports, speeches, posters, on
packaging, even on restroom walls. So I am slowly beginning to treat myself like a beast of burden. I work with
animal sluggishness, chew my food with animal greed, and
doze off with animal resignation before it's time to get
back to work again. I had been conditioned as an animal

for so long that I finally became one. Now they expect no more from me than from an ox. I am deaf to words, even the most beautiful, I don't feel the higher emotions, the higher callings; I don't even know what they are. I do not conceal any dreams which could gladden the Party, government or state. I am an animal; to keep me going on the treadmill, let me gobble my food, empty my bowels, and catch my wind; if not, I will kick out both my hind legs and knock out all the teeth I can, gold teeth, silver teeth, nylon teeth.

Right now, however, I'm in the hospital. A large hospital, a cross between a repair shop and a slaughterhouse. The Party does not poke its nose in here, or rather it does, but uncertainly and without its usual aggressiveness. The Party is a little helpless in this building with its dusty windows; it would like to meddle even in medicine, but fear overcomes it at the last minute because it needs those doctors. Instead, it grabs the professors by their necks for a moment, then lets them go; feeds the proper propaganda to the nurses, then suddenly relents; plasters the operating rooms with slogans, then takes them right back down in fear of germs. More often now, they slip in here on the sly with their Loyal sons whose livers have rotted out from overwork, who have gotten cataracts, or whose blood has gone bad.

A member of the directorate will be operated on tomorrow. But first I will enter the ward guarded by agents and eagerly lend a hand in the preparations. Amid hissing sterilizers, clicking meters, the metallic sighs of resuscitation equipment, in this large green interior which reminds one of the cabin of a spaceship, an intergalactic ship in which the patient will make the shorter or longer flight to God, in this pathetic asepsis I will carry cylinders containing various gases, sprinkle the floor with liquid disinfectants, turn on the hot water for the surgeon's hands, and at the same time I will shoot a quick glance or two over at the large table on which the surgical instruments, disinfected by the hospital staff and the police, lie covered by a sheet; then, in passing, I will carefully lift that sheet and fart with all my might on those sacred instruments, from my apocalyptic anus I will fart a horrendous, mighty stream of gonococci, white spirochetes, golden staphylococci. I will blast out the billions of bacteria and viruses which have built up in me during my decades of disgraceful slavery.

If they had just tortured us with their insolent omnipresence, if they had just buried us in prisons, if they had only just drilled ideological holes in our bellies and brains, if they had just dehumanized us with daily life, betrayals, and venality, if they had only just turned us from a nation into an anonymous horde of animals, but they bore and bore us, bore us to tears, they torment us, drive us crazy with endless talk, piss boring boredom all over us. Boredom comes yawning down from the sky, the trees, the country fields, from the seas and the oceans, the newspapers and theaters, the laboratories and stripteases, from buildings and official limousines, from schoolchildren and the physiognomies of dignitaries. Boredom is the secret elixir of our regime. Boredom is its lover, its mother. Boredom is its natural smell. Boredom emanates from government brains and government traps. Boredom emanates from the military, the police, from listening devices. Boredom seeps from prisons and torture cells. Boredom is their own curse. They are ashamed of that boredom, afraid of it; they choke on it and will never free themselves of it. Boredom is the boundless abyss in which they drown and we drown along with them. Boredom is Satan in earthly form.

Night is falling. Red carpets are being laid down in the hall. On one wall someone hangs a large picture showing the happy life of my adopted country. Serene, majestic music flows from hidden speakers. Night is drawing near and with it the day of my first and final clash with violence, tyranny, hell. The nurses bring tea, the superfluous old man in the corridor is starting to die, but no one believes him or no one has time to believe him. A burly man disguised as an orderly is wandering through the wards. In one spot he bends over a sleeping patient, in another he takes the hand of a man with a fever, elsewhere he collects coins from convalescents. But I know that he is a priest in disguise, a priest of a beleaguered religion who walks among the patients, bringing them a forbidden solace. For that old compromised religion has, as a result of persecution, regained its beauty, its nobility, and become strangely attractive. And so the priest disguised as an orderly, in spite of his corpulence and his cunning eyes, here enjoys the authority of an apostle, a martyr, almost that of a saint. He does not approach me, he only casts me a glance from a distance, but in that glance I read some sort of transcendental understanding between us; him, the messenger of heaven, and me, an emigrant from the first cradle of humanity.

Dear friend, fortunate citizen of fortunate Europe, I bring this letter to a close and fall to my knees so that in the ancient language of my forefathers I can whisper the words of my daily prayer which I composed myself and which I ask you to say for my soul:

O God of the free stars, the free solar winds, the independent universe, holy God of freedom, have pity on us, the unfree, the humiliated, the debased who hang forever suspended between life and death, heaven and hell. Have pity on us and grant us eternal rest from the violence

of our brother, the tyranny of our father, the betrayal of
our son.

*

Someone was pounding a fist on the door, making the
glass rattle under the calico half-curtain.

"Speak up in there! What happened? Why have you
locked the door?" We recognized the manager's angry
voice.

"Nothing happened. The customer was resting," answered Basia, collecting her clothes from the floor.

"Then why is the door closed?"

"There was a draft. Wait a minute, the key fell on the
floor somewhere."

"Hurry up, it's already closing time. We're closing the
store right this minute."

"Coming, coming. One second. I'm helping the customer get himself together."

The manager walked off into the depths of her kingdom, issuing orders like a captain before abandoning a
sinking ship. Basia dressed like a streak of lightning. She
already had on her turtleneck and jeans. She pulled on her
high boots with their miniature spurs. I was trying to keep
up, but things either kept slipping out of my hands or they
went on the wrong way. Basia dressed herself, then me,
with swift, efficient gestures.

"Did I do a good imitation of an earth girl?" she asked
with a sly smile.

She was once again as slender and frail as she'd been
when our acquaintance began.

"Well, anyhow, it was good you led me astray. Now
I'm sorry that you don't go to night school and that you're
not apprenticing in the store."

144

"We'll see about all that. You're going to be late for your Christmas Eve, you poor thing."

"It's my privilege to be late for Christmas Eve. I've made so many long journeys on Christmas Eve and woken up from them in the gutter."

She stopped in front of the door, with the large black key in her long, slender hand that was like a bird's wing. She turned slowly around and looked at me with her large protruding eyes familiar to any connoisseur of Venetian art. And then she asked softly, "And did you wake up in the gutter today, too?"

"No, Basia. I used to wake up in the dumps, but tasteful dumps which, with my fondness for demonic stylization, I called the gutter. On the whole, my gutters have been elegant. I'm an aesthete, Basia. A bashful aesthete."

"I think you'll remember this Christmas Eve for a long time."

"Yes, Basia. I'll remember it as my last happy one. But do you really have any idea who I am?"

"You are an older client who was patiently waiting in line for gold wedding rings."

"That probably doesn't say enough."

"I know how much is enough. Some night when you're home in your little nook and you can't fall asleep and your thoughts are roaming the world visiting your girls, real and imaginary, girls who were swept away by the winds of time and those who have not yet been born and who will most likely never come into this world, there will be a red, glimmering light on in my house. You are under my control. I am your guardian angel."

She turned the key in the lock and opened the door to the dark, cold corridor.

"So, is this the end, then, Basia, my guardian angel?"

"For you it's a relief."

"And an anguish."

145

"There you go again. That's you in a nutshell."

I walked up to her at the threshold of the door, at the border of the rose-colored cave. Before us, the abyss of an unheated jewelry store in a modest metropolis in a socialist state. Sadly I realized that she was half a head taller than I. But that had no meaning now.

"In a few days the earth will begin its four billionth and first orbit of the sun," said Basia. "I wish you a good cosmic journey, my exhausted astronaut."

"How do you know precisely which orbit it's making?"

"That's what they're teaching us in school now."

"And, Basia, I wish you . . . but I don't really know what I wish. Good grades, or a swift broom for distant journeys?"

"Bye, love. Bye, my two-legged vertebrate."

"Bye, my guardian angel from business school."

We kissed fondly like a husband and wife after twenty years of marriage. Basia adjusted my muffler, which had gotten twisted around my neck, then let me know with a wink of an eye that now everything looked right. Then she moved on ahead into the musty darkness of the corridor. She walked without a sign of a care, her left shoulder lowered nonchalantly, her miniature spurs jingling. Cool, bored, indifferent to the stupid world.

The manager was waiting, the door seal in her hand. The seal was a beer bottle cap filled with clay into which a piece of string had been inserted. She was winding a flower-patterned silk kerchief over her brushed-back hair and beckoning impatiently to us.

"Hurry up, my dears, hurry up. The first star's gone out already."

The store was empty. The reflection of a neon sign flashed raspberry-red in the puddle on the floor and then, blinking briefly, went out.

"Should we call an ambulance just to be on the safe side?" she asked, struggling with the lock.

"No, thanks. Everything's all right now."

"Can you make it on your own?"

"I can. I don't have far to go."

"If those rings come, I'll put a couple aside for you."

"God bless you. But where's Basia?"

"Basia who?"

"The girl who took care of me."

"Probably far away by now. That's how they are nowadays. Merry Christmas."

"Merry Christmas to you."

I went outside where, to my surprise, it felt like early spring. It was raining, the gutters roared with foaming water, and a wild wind blew headlong down to the river. I raised my eyes to check if there really were no stars. All I saw was a wet darkness tinged pink from beneath by invisible neon.

A police van came chugging down the street. The driver, a burly sergeant, leaned out the side window, scowled at me, and said, "Time to be getting home, Mr. Konwicki. Your family and Christmas Eve are waiting for you."

"Sure, sure, I'm on my way."

"Fine, just so we don't run into you again."

The avenue was deserted all the way down to the Vistula except for the wind-filled rain and the springlike torrents building up and gurgling by the clogged drains. No, there was still a belated little flock of starlings flying skittishly over the streets. The windows glowed with Christmas-tree lights.

Some poor woman with an umbrella was pushing a baby carriage which contained the legless veteran under a blanket. He had finished his day's work and was now returning home for dinner. Recognizing me, he doffed his fur cap.

"Merry Christmas," he said politely.

"Merry Christmas to you and a happy New Year."

"Next year'll definitely be better. I did my horoscope."

"Horoscopes are always good; it's life that doesn't work out."

"Maybe life could be all right, but there's too many of us. There's not enough stars to go round to make a fate for everyone."

He was right, that man the size of a vase. There's no way to quarrel with destiny in such crowded conditions. We saluted each other with raised hands. I glanced after them for a moment as they plunged away into the watery darkness of the street. The woman struggled with the carriage at the crossing, where the curbs were high. Fortunately, a police patrol approached and two young policemen carried the little conveyance over the torrential gutters.

I turned into a side street where Grzesio, wrapped in his scanty denim outfit, was waiting for me.

"Please come with me," he said officiously.

"For what?"

"You'll find out in a minute. It's not far. Just the other side of the street."

We jumped out into the kasha-like mush of the road. Grzesio kept looking back at me as if he was afraid I might suddenly disappear. "I've called you up many times," he said confidentially.

"I don't recall that."

"I did it anonymously. As a reader."

"Were you the one who called me a foreign agent and a Zionist?"

"It was," said Grzesio with a hint of pride. "I'm very happy that we're getting to know each other personally."

He led me up to a heavy gate which led to clean, neat stairs adorned with climbing vines. I could hear the unobtrusive sound of an accordion and was enveloped by the blissful warmth of a well-working radiator. The sharp, foresty aroma of a Christmas tree hung in the air.

Kojran emerged from the half light. "She's a sly bitch, that one, closes up shop to get rid of us."

"Who?"

"The manager, that's who. You'll see, the goods'll arrive any minute now. She has her own special customers. The Russians must be hiding, waiting somewhere."

"That's a fact," added Duszek. "They can wait because they don't celebrate Christmas Eve."

"But I saw her seal the door," I said irritably.

"She can seal herself up, for all I care, but you know, if the goods went out they've got to arrive. Why waste words. We'll see who can outwait who."

Then he showed me the landing of an elegant staircase, an amphitheater in the discreet darkness. There, in careless poses, sitting, half-lying, my old acquaintances were encamped—the woman in the pelisse, the student and the anarchist, the peasant woman, Grzesio, and that old woman who had proven not to be so old and who was now sitting on the lap of one of the construction workers. A little off to one side, sitting like Rejtan in the famous portrait, an accordionist from a street band had found himself a spot. He was leaning up against the unfastened front of his accordion, his fingers wandering along the keyboard, listening intently to his own improvisations. A real Christmas tree stood on the top step.

"Feeling better?"

"Yes, I'm feeling good again."

"You know the best way to a woman."

"Kojran, you really don't believe I was feeling sick?"

"Ah, you're such a faker. You were just after Iwona."

"Her name's Basia, not Iwona."

"What do you mean, Basia? I've known her by sight for six months. It's Iwona, she lives over in Latawiec. Now maybe you're going to swear you didn't get in?"

"Kojran, I'm a seriously ill person."

"Come on, swear."

"What do I have to swear for? I want to go home and get into my own bed."

"God, what did she see in you?"

"She didn't see anything. She was just helping someone who felt bad."

"C'mon. You need a good smack in the chops."

"Why is it you envy me, Kojran? Come on, let's change lives. I'll fly off to America tomorrow instead of you and you can go to Kalisz after the holidays. You can see thousand-year-old relics, go to court, and meet a man who's hated you with a passion for ten years. Take my coat and go to my house. To a chilly stabilization before a not-too-distant freeze-up."

"You sound like you're reading from one of your own books, goddamnit."

There was a little stir on the staircase. The anarchist got up from his terrazzo, his shirt unbuttoned to the waist, his bristly blond chest hair gleaming damply. He walked over to us and pulled a small, rusty box from his pocket.

"Shall we have a little smoke?" he asked. "Good stuff."

He opened the lid. The box contained thin, handmade joints nicely rolled in light-blue paper.

"Take one," he said, offering them to me and Kojran.

We lit one up while he treated the others.

"What is that?" said Duszek. "It smells funny."

"A souvenir from Carlos." The anarchist laughed confidentially.

"Carlos who?" pressed Duszek.

"Just inhale and don't ask questions. We'll explain when the time comes."

The red coals of cigarettes glowed on the stairs. The old woman who had turned out not to be so old was whispering in the construction worker's ear. He was shivering from the cold, still wearing his work clothes, his labor insignia on his chest, the letter B formed of brick arches. The others were now treating them with discreet understanding, as if they were already engaged.

"Oh, Goska, Goska," sighed the worker, his teeth chattering.

Perhaps he felt like going back home and putting on a warm sweater, but since that was not to be, he'd given himself over to this romance sudden as a spring storm. They were sharing a cigarette.

"There was a time when I had to read you," said the peasant woman apropos of nothing as she emerged from behind the bannister. She unbuttoned her caracul coat, revealing a silvery evening gown.

"And why was it that you had to read me, lovely lady?" I asked with a feeling of familiar sadness.

"You were required reading until they scratched you off the list. It was something about a construction project. Production reportage. Horribly boring stuff."

"I beg your pardon. I fall to your feet and beg your pardon. But, as I remember, it was short and rather humorous."

"Not that short, and horribly boring."

"You're fooling me now, you crone."

"What are you saying?"

"I'm saying that was all a very long time ago. Better not to admit how long. For you or me, either."

"But you were a socialist-realist, right?"

"I was, my cow."

"You're a hack."

"No, I'm not, it's just that my head is reeling."

Just then Kojran walked over with his inseparable companion, Duszek. They were greedily puffing on their joints.

"What is this stuff he's given us?"

"That's the smell of freedom, the aroma of a distant land," called out the student sprawled beneath the Christmas tree.

"Brother Konwicki, he's poisoning us, that terrorist."

"But you're smoking."

"I like the taste."

"I like the taste, too. But I better lie down. I'm losing my balance."

"That's what it does," muttered the student. "Hosanna."

"Konwa, why are you standing there without saying a word?"

"When a Pole gets laid, he gets worried," stated Duszek.

"I have to go home," I said.

"So go."

"I don't feel like it. Did you hear organs playing?"

"What organs? That's an accordion. Duszek, what was it I was supposed to remember?"

"The present from his cousin."

"Right. You see, that Soviet tourist left you a keepsake. He went through his pockets and he started getting worried. He wanted to leave you something posh. And this is what he left."

Kojran opened his shoulder bag and withdrew an oblong piece of malachite. I recognized that greenish-black rod resembling an old carbine shell eaten by green rust. I used to see it in a drawer at my house. And now it had caught up with me later in life.

"Well," Kojran pressed me, "what does it do?"

"Nothing. Just an old family memento."

"I wanted to give him your address, but he didn't want it."

"I didn't want his address, either."

"A strange family, I swear to God. That thing have any gold in it?"

"No, it's rock. There are rocks like this around Lake Baikal. A lake bigger than a sea."

With some difficulty I walked deeper into the gateway, where a yellow bulb glowed beneath frosted glass. So, it was the same rock a grandfather or perhaps a great-grandfather of mine had brought back from exile. I remembered something, but what I did remember was mixed in with what I'd read. There was some sort of a revolt by the Polish exiles who were building a road near Baikal. The prisoners' conspiracy ended, as usual, in failure. An ill-fated impulse which left behind a life-giving legend.

Yes, it was that same stone, signifying nothing in my childhood. A black-veined green stone on whose reverse side someone had etched the image of an eagle with outspread wings, a primitive likeness of the bird of freedom. That bird was black because a hundred years' worth of ink had carbonized in the grooves but, pressed onto paper, it would leave the white shadow of that freedom-loving bird.

Kojran staggered over, leading Duszek. "I was supposed to tell you about him when the time came. He runs a commission counter in Hala Mirowska. But at one time he worked with the secret police."

"I'm sick of hearing about that." Duszek spat. "He starts drinking and everything comes back to him. It's been twenty years already."

"That's because I'm carrying your absolution right here in my heart. But I won't absolve you now, Duszek, maybe tomorrow, at the airport."

Kojran's gaping eyes squinted at his inseparable tormentor, or his inseparable victim.

"It's you who's driving me to America!"

"Shhh. Shut your trap. You see that night crawler following us." Duszek pointed at Grzesio, who was lying lifelessly right there on the first step.

"Boy, did he pamper me, I swear to God, there's probably nobody gets pampered like that anywhere today. I'll show you. I just have to unbutton my shirt."

"Enough. That's it. No one here's interested." Duszek grabbed his friend with his powerful arms and forced him to button his shirt.

"But when the secret police let him go, he fastened on to me, and he's waiting for absolution for those old sins of his."

"You've sinned, I've sinned, and so has Konwicki. The whole world is sinful."

They were both plucking at me as if I were a judge seeking out justice. But within myself I heard the heavy, massive voice of a harmonium.

"Let's go lie down," I said. "That anarchist's given us lovage weed."

"Young people smoke strong cigarettes these days."

"If we lie down, we won't get back up," complained Kojran.

"That would be good—to lie down and never get back up," I whispered, searching for a comfortable spot at the feet of the construction worker and Goska, who, their hands linked, were staring straight ahead as if seeing a city on fire, a sea parting, manna falling from heaven.

There was a large package wrapped in brown paper by the bannister. Whatever was inside shone with a silvery, festive, expensive gleam. I tore off a loose strip of the packing paper to reveal a large, gleaming electric samovar.

"Whose is this?" I asked.

Kojran sat down inertly beside me. "Mine. I had to buy something."

"He won the trip to Russia," piped up the woman in the pelisse. "When your luck's running, you can't lose. Show him the sales slip."

Kojran fumbled inside his shirt. "What do I need the trip for? What am I, a Boy Scout? For God's sake, tell me, where should I go? Ask the anarchist."

The student consulted with his comrade while Kojran took out the lucky sales slip and checked it under the light.

"Take a look, goddamnit. A number with a thirteen in it and it wins. I'm always lucky when it comes to this kind of thing."

"Don't worry. Could be a mistake," I said.

"What kind of mistake? The manager phoned the head office. They checked the list. No two ways about it."

With the last of his strength the student crawled over to our step. "He says better a week in Russia than a whole life in America."

"He could be well informed," said Kojran, now having some doubts.

"Yes, he did visit America."

"But did he visit Russia?"

"That I can't say."

The accordionist was leisurely dragging out some ominous oratorio. The construction worker had plunged his work-wearied hand under the not-that-old Goska's skirt. The steps looked as if they led to the stars.

Kojran folded the sales slip in four and put it away in his shoulder bag. Then, with some effort, he beckoned with his pale hand to Grzesio. "Come here, would you, son."

But Grzesio had weakened, too, and wobbled over to

our loge. "Be good enough to go outside and see what's happening at the store. They might be bringing the shipment in through the back."

"But this is Christmas Eve, Tadeusz," said the young man, trying to wriggle out of it.

"Christmas Eve's the best time for mischief."

And so, reluctantly, Grzesio set out for the deep shadow of the gateway, where spring hurricane winds were now swirling.

"Your name is Tadeusz, too?" I asked Kojran, surprised.

"That's right, mine too."

"That's odd."

"What's so odd about it? Around here every other person's named Tadeusz. But it is odd. Ought to be, anyway."

"Maybe it's normal. Just give me your tickets to America and we'll make Christmas tree ornaments out of them. Your lucky sales slip is enough for you. Make the trip, have a look around, then come back so you and I can drink half a liter of Moscow vodka. Why take any chances, if it's no better than regular everyday life here?"

"Listen to what happened to me, Konwa. I was once the boy from the fairy tale. I was Janek the musician, the sorcerer's apprentice, a young Byron. How did I hit the skids? What was the mix-up that left me a primitive old codger? Must have been a lack of training. My consciousness, my perception system, my sensibility, the tendons of my soul, the lenses of my clairvoyance, they all remained dormant. I never practiced or perfected or encouraged any of it. And that's why it withered away and died in me before I was even dead myself. I condemned myself to an animal existence. Or could that have been fate?"

"Listen to you. You've got a long journey ahead. Either to the East or to the West," I said drowsily.

"You Nobel Prize asshole," grumbled Kojran. "I haven't got the strength to get up and kick that literary ass of yours."

The student ground out his butt on the dark-blue wainscoting, listening to the mutterings of the foreign prophet, who was rubbing his yellowish chest and staring up at the slanted ceiling or the unseeable sky beyond it.

"He says," translated the student softly, "that all previous forms for organizing society have outlived their time. He says that every government, consciously or unconsciously, makes every effort to improve its exercise of power. Thus, the goal of every government is total, unrestrained totalitarian dictatorship. If this goal has not been fulfilled everywhere, it's only because it is opposed by old democratic and liberal habits which are growing frailer all the time, waning by the day, habits which once, in a few places, were vitally alive and had taken the form of constitutional, parliamentary, and social institutions. Every president of a democratic state who by day blithers on about the freedom of the individual, the parliamentary system, and the rule of law, writhes at night in paroxysms of envy for the president of the neighboring country who has ordered himself elected for life, introduced censorship and summary justice, and who rules by decree. So, at night he dreams heavenly dreams of the happy day when he will be able to dissolve parliament, tap everyone's phone, beef up the secret police, build concentration camps, and declare himself a god. If one can assume the existence of an international proletariat, one can be all the more certain of the healthy existence of an internationale of presidents, chiefs, juntas, tyrants, and dictators. If we believe in the International Red Cross, how much easier to convince ourselves of the workings of an international secret police which furthers the conspiracies of the tyrants. Let us not be deceived by the insults bandied about by heads of state

157

and national leaders, let us not be beguiled by police actions and military incidents. Let us not be taken in by ideological campaigns played out before our eyes between political blocs or social systems. All of this is opium for the masses. It's all a big show for little innocent children. A carnival for the world, while despots, greedy for unlimited godlike power, carry out coup d'états, coups against our dignity, our freedom, human life."

Grzesio emerged from the dark, brushing the rain off himself. Even at a distance he gave off a smell of wind and water.

"What are you reading?" he asked the student. "Where was it published?"

"You're a real thoroughbred stoolie." Duszek laughed good-naturedly. Grzesio got on his nerves, though he often found something touching about him as well.

"The store is closed for good," Grzesio reported. "It won't open again till Judgment Day."

"You won't be buying your rings," said Kojran sleepily.

"No, I won't." I sighed.

"What is it, some sort of anniversary?"

"No. Nothing significant. For once in my life, especially now toward the end, I want to do the unexpected. I want a totally unmotivated impulse, an adventure, like cracking up a car."

The peasant woman was undoing her sack, looking for something. A moment later she was putting candles and strings of sparklers on the Christmas tree. Left ajar, the gate slammed deliberately against the gate frame. The wind was racing wildly up and down the empty avenue.

"How about you?" I asked the student. "You lead him around like a blind man or Wernyhora the blind singer. What about you, you yourself?"

"I don't know yet. I didn't study in the beginning. I avoided mastering all the bullshit. I told myself: I won't cram in all that, it's garbage, a convention, a government liturgy, so I didn't read because it's just crap they ram down your throat. That was my modest little program, not to swallow any of the castor oil forced on me, even though it'd mean not passing my finals and messing up my studies. I took care of myself, I have a light, empty stomach, I can digest anything worth digesting. I'm pure, you can buy me."

"He's for sale, too," acknowledged Kojran, glancing over at me with a porcelain eye.

"I used to be for sale, but those days are past."

"Don't make us any sadder, goddamnit, write something to give us strength."

The terrorist approached the peasant woman, who had tossed off her caracul fur coat and was now struggling with a box of wet matches. They worked together, striking the state match monopoly's inferior products. Finally, a small bluish flame flared up and began to bite at the chilled candles. The terrorist, touched by this archaic ritual, laid his large, dark hand on the peasant woman's hip. With a skillful movement of her waist, she shook the alien burden off. The terrorist was trying to explain something.

"He says," translated the student, "that he has a constant hard-on. Night and day since he was fifteen."

"What concern is that of ours? Let him see a doctor," said the peasant woman haughtily.

"He's seen plenty. None of them could help him."

"What nonsense. Who's supposed to believe that?" said Duszek irritably.

"He says it's the truth. He even wants to show you. He suffers a lot."

"He'll get no cure for it from me," snorted the peasant woman who had been a cabaret actress at one time.

"Perhaps you might be interested?" the student asked the woman in the pelisse.

"Just you be careful or I'll call the police."

At that moment the gate gave a groan as if it had been sawed in half. Measured steps and a nose being blown could be heard in the dark. Two young policemen suffering from head colds appeared before us.

"Good evening," said the one in charge, who had three stripes. "May I know the purpose of this gathering?"

"We're going visiting. For Christmas Eve," said Duszek.

"We sat down to rest because the elevator's not working," added Kojran.

"And who are you visiting?"

Startled, none of us said a word. The little candle flames on the Christmas tree showed signs of anxiety as well. The policeman with the three stripes peered at each of us in turn with his watery eyes.

"Who are you paying a Christmas call on?"

Grzesio turned over on his other side. "To Mr. Nowak. In number seventeen."

The policeman appraised his rain-dampened jeans. "Your papers, please."

Grzesio automatically reached for his side pants pocket, but then caught himself and pulled out his crumpled ID from his breast pocket.

"He was about to show his badge," snickered Duszek. "He's still a young pigeon."

The senior policeman took down poor Grzesio's information while the other one looked at us with the red, exhausted eyes of a sick rabbit. The accordion player was practicing some sort of dodecaphony interwoven with the indeterminent whistling of bellows. Finally, the policeman returned Grzesio's documents and said, "Please be off for your visit and refrain from any further assemblies. Happy holidays."

"All the best to you." Duszek bowed.

The policemen set off toward the gate with a measured stride.

"They took your name down," said the student with satisfaction. "We'll be next to each other in the records."

"Let them write what they want, two-bit coppers."

The terrorist lit a sparkler, the starlike sparks showering onto the terrazzo floor, which in the night resembled Carrara marble. The construction worker and Goska were in each other's arms by the balustrade. They seemed to be dozing, but something was jolting them, for, after a few moments of standing still, they began struggling as if to free themselves from some invisible bonds. Through the broken glass of a mezzanine window the ragged walls of an old, half-destroyed building could be seen. Christmas trees glowed in the apartments that had survived.

It was only then that I noticed that the student's thin face with its meager beard and spotty mustache resembled the face of Christ, as all the faces of young people seem to in my old age. Have they taken on the features of that man martyred so long ago or has Christ himself returned in this age of greatest crisis, an age which needs a Christ or, at least, a Mephisto.

"You swine!" said Duszek, raising his voice. "You were screwing the lady on the steps."

The construction worker released Goska from his arms, straightened his clothes, flicking some pine needles from his work jacket with its emblem of brick arches.

"What? What? Who are you jumping on?"

"I saw everything, you swine. What's the matter, you blind? She's an old woman, you ought to be ashamed of yourself, goddamnit."

"Forget the old business," said Goska, rising from the heated step. "I could be your daughter. You can see what kind of body I still have."

"If she has a body," hissed the peasant woman furiously, "then what is it I have?"

She started to open the zipper of her silver lamé evening dress. The anarchist rushed over to assist her.

"Get your paws off me. I can do it myself. Let that writer compare the two of us."

"Why me? I'm nearsighted."

"But with the help of that secretary, you found your way to the back of the store all right."

"My heart was on the blink. I'm saying farewell to this world, my good woman."

"You'll outlive us all. You'll have to be put to sleep at state expense in the next century."

"Why are you so unfriendly to me?"

"You know why."

"Because of one lousy book, my queen?"

"There's a hundred reasons. And every one is like a flower, a flower of evil."

"My God, but you're well read."

"Come here."

"I'm afraid to. I better not."

Kojran opened his eyes. He was staring at a point above the wainscoting where the small galaxy of an ant collective stretched in monotonous rhythm along the lichen-covered wall. The small, indestructible ants of some pharaoh coming out from somewhere to conquer a civilization. A civilization which had lost faith in itself.

"Quiet, listen," whispered Kojran.

We all fell silent without a murmur of dissent. The peasant woman's hand froze as if her half-open zipper were a holster. The candles and branches swayed together in the strange vertical drafts.

"What is it?" I asked.

Kojran closed his eyes, then opened them languidly. "Children singing Christmas carols."

And, in fact, there was an angelic choir somewhere; children's voices always seem celestial to us.

"Goddamnit, somehow it makes me feel sorry."

"Sorry about what?"

"Doesn't matter what. Terribly sorry. I heard carols in the woods with the partisans. I heard them in prisons and I heard them with whores, but I never heard any that sounded like that."

"Maybe even you are believing in miracles now?"

"What kind of miracles?"

"The kind that can never happen and never will."

"To who?"

"To us here, us in general."

It seemed to me the singing fell from somewhere above us, from the heights of a stairwell in some mysterious house. I rose to my feet, stepped over Goska's and the construction worker's legs, and walked past the anarchist, who was fingering Buddhist rosary beads. The stairs grew darker as I climbed, the caroling louder. But it was not a carol. The singing held too much complaint, too many unwept tears.

In total darkness I sought the wall. Cold, slimy, like the Great Wall of China, it rose toward unseen hills. Now I could hear the winds running riot on that crook-backed hill, scattering the cheerless singing of those angelic voices like mist.

My fingers discovered a wooden door frame snarled with knots of oak. I also found the door handle, huge, brass, saturated with the warmth of the hands which had recently grasped it. I opened the door which a second before was black as blindness.

And then I was on the threshold of a chapel lit with the bluish light of electric lamps like lilies of the valley. Women wearing different-colored hospital robes were sitting on the benches in front of me. I saw a few men, also in hospital dress. Here and there the top of a crutch jutted above the bench. Two pale girls with thick candles in their hands were standing by the altar. They were looking at a young Dominican intoning the versicles of the litany. Beside me, her thin hands on her yellowed accordion, an old nun accompanied the faithful's responses to the litany.

I saw the jug of holy water, the container of holy oil. The girls took the cross from the hands of the young priest. They were his age, yet they called him father.

To my left the black wood of a confessional. The end of a violet stole hung down from the sill of the little door. A round, old face wearing pince-nez or perhaps eyeglasses loomed within. The anonymous, everyday face of a person waiting for someone.

I was certain he was looking at my back. Looking at me, thinking about me—perhaps as a priest or as an ordinary person bored by the winter evening.

Suddenly I turned, walked over to the confessional, and knelt on the smoothly worn step. There was a black wooden grating in front of me. His strange presence. He was aware of me, I of him. I didn't know how to begin.

The litany had ended. A young monk came out behind the small altar the size of a garden table. He was going to say Mass for the converts.

"Father," I whispered, "I have not been at confession for a long time. Twenty, thirty years."

For a moment neither of us said anything.

"I am listening. Speak," whispered the person behind the grating.

"In those years I have sinned like everybody else. I lied. I was envious, I denied God."

I broke off for a moment and then added, "And I committed adultery."

"Go on," that shadow of a human presence encouraged me.

164

These are the sins of my childhood and my youth. I counted them off every month in a little wooden church near Wilno. They were heard by Father Pereswiet-Soltan, who is no longer alive. He died in his own bed or was tortured to death by atheists. But what sins have I committed as an adult?

I lied, was jealous, I committed adultery, kept losing faith and rediscovering it, but are those sins, is God interested in them, aren't they just our daily routine, the sad statistics of human existence? But still I feel guilty, keenly, painfully guilty before my times and before God. But I am not sure of God because, in our defective human imagination, He appears driven by fear, uncertainty, and despair, and I do not understand my times because I have seen them only in the twinkling of my fifty years.

Where does my guilt come from? From my character or my fear-choked sense of life's unpredictability? From a greedy need to know and understand what cannot be known or understood, or from forgetting my obligations to the people who speak the same language I do and with whom I shuffle in a line that leads toward an ominous future.

The monk flashed the bared chalice. The pale girls stood motionlessly, protecting the candles' frail flames. The harmonium spoke with a short-winded sigh and then, in sudden fear, fell silent. Portraits of the students were hung between the tall windows, the face of contemporary youth. The bearded faces of the God-Man. Ribonucleic acid confirms his humanity. And his divinity is guaranteed by the ebb and flow of hope like the violent gusts of solar wind.

Where do my faults come from? From the aggression of my fellow men, from some sense of original sin committed in the universe by beings from whom I inherited the neutrons of my flesh, the energy of my soul? Perhaps I am guilty before my own fate for not fulfilling and realizing it,

165

because I sabotage destiny in every instant of my daily life, enticed by my own consciousness, which breaks its bonds, eludes my control, and floats away like a cloud of narcotic smoke into the moral void above us.

"Speak. I am listening," repeated Father Pereswiet-Soltan.

No. I want my guilt to be as simple as possible. I want to stand guilty before people unknown to me, people who drowned in the sea of anonymity fulfilling their tough human duty, people who, in the darkness of despair, barred the roads against the floodwaters of evil, time, or history with their own bones, who in pain and labor gave birth to me so that I could shout as loud as I could, so that I could howl to the very ends of heaven and earth, so that I could save myself and God.

*

The modern world's unfreedom brings to mind certain situations from crime films: the telephone rings, the criminal orders the kidnapped victim to pick up the receiver and speak with the caller in a normal, friendly tone of voice. Or, unexpectedly, someone enters a house taken over by criminals. The person who lives there, aware of the hidden bandits' pistols trained on him, receives his guest as if nothing at all were wrong, fixes him a drink, tries to act normal, and as quickly as possible drives away the one person who might have been able to help him. Or, bandits fleeing from a bank push a terrified woman teller out in front of them, using her body as a shield as they run to their car. The woman begs the guardians of justice not to shoot and to let the bandits make a safe getaway.

That's how it is with entire nations in today's world. Where are the beautiful times of old-fashioned slavery? Where is the battle of the invader with the language of the oppressed, with their emblems of state; where are the open, ceremonial persecutions of patriots; where are the solemn executions of heroes? That slavery, in retrospect, was open, theatrical, celebrational. And everyone knew who was coercing the weak and who would answer to the court of history for that coercion.

Today slavery has become invisible. On the surface some poor nation behaves naturally, listens with reverence to its own anthem, elects a parliament, dispatches emissaries, sits on the Security Council; in a word, acts like any independent, sovereign state. And not one sees the revolver at its back, a cocked revolver belonging to its neighbor or to some other country. A nation of this sort utters businesslike, thoughtful, even profound speeches with a poker face and no one could guess that, with all its strength, from the marrow out, it wants to roar like a beast whose throat is being cut, screech like a rabbit being skinned, howl to God for help against inevitable doom.

Previously, a slave was entitled to cry out; today the slave has been assured the right of silence, muteness. Crying out brought relief, as it does for a newborn baby. Silence and muteness cause degeneration, they suffocate, kill. Previously, when a captive nation regained its freedom, it was not hindered in joining the great family of free nations. Today, if by chance it is set free, it will no longer be fit for life and will perish from the poisons accumulated during the dark night of captivity.

The world is undergoing a great crisis. A crisis of philosophy, ethics, customs, culture, environment, collective and individual self-consciousness. Imagine the form this crisis takes in a country whose situation is already critical, a state which is in its final agony illuminated by its obvious slavery. If certain human criteria have faded away in the world, in the captive nations, no one even remembers what they once were. If morality has wavered in the free countries, it has long since been ground into dust among the captives. If art has grown stranded in certain places, it has been transformed into a louse among the unfree. And that louse, I add for my own part, loves to adopt fashionable poses, rebellious gestures, universal expressions. Remember that.

Let me see now, I meant to say something else. I did have something else in mind. I've lost the thread again, as I always do. But now I'm losing it more and more often. No doubt I was thinking about forced elections, that blasted moral balloting to which whole generations are subjected, every individual, every poor innocent man in the street. In the world of the unfree there are permanent choices of behavior vis-à-vis the authorities, their coercion, caprices, and crimes. One has to settle one's accounts with conscience on a daily basis; every day the two courts of the devil and the Lord God sentence us to a short eternity until the next reckoning.

But it was another problem I wanted to raise. I can envision something I am unable to make clear. I remember certain moments from my childhood, in winter perhaps, or in spring—tragic moments in my foolish life or in my family's fate. I see my grandmother's face, the face of a woman no longer young, a face lined with tectonic, orogenic, or perhaps seismic metamorphoses. I am startled when that face shrivels, and is soiled with new wrinkles, when that face so familiar, so well remembered, when that mirror dims with the unexpected ugliness of despair, hideous unhappiness, the abomination of pain; when troubled tears roll down that landscape of woe, I choke with laughter, I flee from myself and give out my last gasp of laughter.

Now, however, I frighten people with the face of my late grandmother. All God's creation flees me. Foreigners loathe me because I reek of slavery, and the whole street laughs at me because shameless tears flow from my bleary eyes; someone kicks my butt because my misshapen, miserable existence blocks his sun.

Now I know there's more to it than that. I dreamed of writing a treatise on tragedy and buffoonery. In our country tragedy often walks hand in hand with buffoonery. In this I see our strength. I love that ambiguous consanguinity, that risky symbiosis, that genius of a people enchanted in two directions. Our tragic nature is opalescent, its unclear colors keep changing, it gurgles shamelessly, reaches limits bordering on unctuousness, chokes on hysterical giggles. Our buffoonery has a sob in its throat, our buffoonery gnaws its fingers till they bleed, our buffoonery ties the rope around its own neck.

Let's stop. I've remembered what I wanted to proclaim. At last the new idea I was holding in reserve has surfaced to consciousness. Yes, I was running to you with a call to arms and I can't go the distance. The earth has lost one second. This year, in its monotonous cosmic journey in the bowels of the galaxy, the third planet of this solar system experienced the cataclysm of falling behind one infinitely long instant of time. That second is a hair torn from the beard of an unrecognized God. The god of time.

What meaning does this have for people? What meaning for me?

*

Somebody was patting my cheek. I felt soft, cold fingers meting out punishment or treating me to an untimely caress.

"Sleeping on other people's stairs?"

"What happened?"

"That's what I'm asking you. You disappeared for half an hour. You feeling ill?"

169

"Is that you, Basia?"

"No. Julia."

"Julia who?"

"Julia from before."

I picked myself up from the stairs and saw before me in the dark the peasant woman, again wrapped in her molting caracul coat.

"I have a headache," I said. "Those French cigarettes weren't so good for our health."

"Basia—is that the girl from the jewelry store?"

No doubt she had been a great beauty during the cold war. Even now the hard lines of her makeup held the fading beauty of a rock-hard Polish blond. Women of that sort have afforded me many surprises.

"Basia's gone, gone for good," I sighed melancholically.

"You look like the amorous type to me."

"Just appearances, Julia, a distortion from what you read of me in school."

"Your feelings are hurt. Lots of pretty girls cursed that tripe of yours in high school."

"What is this, everybody reads my lousy books and no one reads the good ones?"

"Lots of people dislike you. And women aren't the best when it comes to remembering things."

"So you know something about my women, too?"

"I've heard a thing or two. You did a little poaching in Warsaw's left bank in your day."

"I thought people would have forgotten by now."

"People yes, but women no. They complain it wasn't any good with you."

"I did my best."

The distant choir could again be heard, as if coming from a neighboring town or the depths of the forest.

"They're singing carols," I said in astonishment.

"It is Christmas Eve."

"Yes, that's true."

I went back down the stairs to where the jewelry store line continued its lethargic existence near the broken elevator with its one small, red, blurred window. The candles had already burned halfway down and long white drops of congealed paraffin dotted the branches.

"Where were you, Mr. K.?" asked Kojran sleepily.

"I went to confession."

"Feel better?"

"Hard to say."

"I went yesterday and I feel better."

"Look, your samovar is rusting."

Kojran drew the great, half-wrapped, nickel-plated thing over to him, examined it with care, and began rubbing its swelling sides with his sleeve.

"That's not rust," he mumbled, reassured. "It's blood."

"Whose?"

"Grzesio's. Or the student's. They got into a fight while you were gone."

"Over what?"

"Over nothing. They just started hitting each other."

Grzesio was lying nearby, on the third step up. Holding a handkerchief to his nose, he was staring goggle-eyed into the abyss of the many-storied stairwell. The student was whispering with the anarchist. There was no sign of the fight on him. Life's sharp edges make no dents in those lean, sinewy types.

"Where are you going?"

"To see if it's worth waiting."

"Waiting for what?"

"The goods. The delivery of the Soviet rings."

"Ah yes." Kojran shook his head. "See, your memory's better than mine."

Ice creaked beneath our feet in the great hallway.

A biting wind slashed from wall to wall, and had already torn down announcements from the block housing, tenant, and arbitration committees. The entire public life of a Warsaw apartment building was being buffeted about on the ground.

I pushed open the ancient wings of the gate. Rattling sorrowfully, it rolled open and struck up against a glass case containing a woman's hat covered by a piece of riddled plastic, a Varsovian Tiffany promoting his goods by the exit of our little retreat. To my horror I saw a trapped fly struggling in that glass cell lit and warmed by a bare bulb, that dusty rectangular microcosm. The fly wanted to escape to freedom, not realizing that death awaited it there.

Somehow the atmosphere had changed. I probably hadn't seen such transparent air since childhood, since those biting cold winter nights in Wilno. It had stopped raining and the new frost creaked like crickets. The last of the melted snow was running down into the drains. A Christmas tree several stories high stood motionlessly in the traffic circle. The wind had already broken most of the tree's colored bulbs. But, in recompense, the sputtering short circuits shone with a copious red. Something had occurred in that lignin which envelops our world, a world beginning its four billion and first orbit around a star called the sun.

I saw my reflection in a constellation of cracked mirrors in a tailors' cooperative. An elderly man wearing crumpled trousers and a thick sheepskin coat. A miserable creature with emphysema of the soul. An intelligent creature with the cancer of the consciousness of existence.

Let me see, how did my confession go? Did I confess all that I had to or just what I wished to, did I settle accounts with my conscience, and plan a revised account, an outline for a poetic self-criticism?

Something was glimmering between the massif of the avenue and the peaked top of the Palace of Culture. It looked like the light of a plane landing.

But no one had absolved me, no one had assigned me any penance. I don't remember if in the darkness of the confessional that shadow of a human being had whispered those ancient words: *"Ego te absolvo,"* if that shadow had knocked soundlessly on the wall of the confessional, at that oak-walled cell, if that shadow had draped that little door with his violet stole bearing the sign of our faith, a sign which could be sent out into intergalactic space, a code for human existence, human anguish.

But it was not the landing lights of a plane in a holding pattern. Though its position kept changing, it remained above the avenue. It zigzagged off toward the roofs of Viennese Secession–style apartments and then after a while returned to its former position again, to dart into the shadow of the Palace of Culture. The light reminded me of a star flattened out like a coin, with its edge toward me, and from that illuminated edge a small stream of red light rose into the night sky like a sail. And that cosmic sail fluttered left and right like the flame of a Christmas tree candle. Then, suddenly, it looked like the flame from the rocket engine of an unidentified flying object.

I surveyed the sky carefully, with no sense of panic. There were many stars. Sparkling as in old poems. Stars don't behave like that these days. Which was why I sensed a certain strange unrest in the space above the crouching city. A singular night was drawing near. That singular night could attract an unidentified flying object (which I don't believe in) which was rising over the avenue and looking down at an obscure Central European city.

I returned to the hallway and my friends. "Come on. I'll show you something."

"What are you going to show us?" asked Kojran.

"Something worth seeing. I give you my word."

"The star of Bethlehem?"

"It could be a star and it could be a space probe."

They followed me out to the frozen street. A police siren was wailing somewhere in the viscera of the city. I stood without saying anything and waited.

"Yes, that's the morning star. Or, to put it simply, our neighbor Venus," said Kojran in a sober tone of voice.

"But it's shining so brightly," marveled Grzesio, the handkerchief still at his nose. "I never saw a star like that."

"Look, it darted to the left!" cried Goska.

"Oh, and now it's gone down."

"You know what, I'll go get the anarchist," decided the student. "He took two years of astronomy."

He returned with the stocky foreigner, who puffed himself up but more from anxiety than from a sense of well-being.

"He says it's Venus," translated the student. "At this time of year Venus appears in that part of the sky and moves quickly east, staying low over the northern horizon."

Disappointed, we said nothing. People were singing Christmas carols in the apartments above the deserted jewelry store on the other side of the street. Somewhere a curtain had caught on fire from a Christmas tree, pieces of broken window glass were falling, someone was calling for help. But we continued to stare at that crack of glaring light with its purple plume.

The terrorist cupped his hands and held them to his eyes like binoculars and whispered something to the student.

"He says it isn't Venus, after all."

"Maybe it's a space probe or an American balloon?" I asked timidly.

"And just why does it have to be American?" said the woman in the pelisse.

"All right, then, what kind?"

"Anyway, it's nothing," she replied angrily. "Why are you pestering me with all this?"

"He says . . ." mumbled the student.

"What does he say?" asked Kojran, growing flustered.

"He says he doesn't know. The phenomenon looks like an unidentified flying object."

Julia, the peasant woman, was shivering, either from the cold or from some astronomical emotion. Looking up at the astral light, she said softly, "Have I offended you?"

"Have I offended you?"

"You know what, I'm inviting you to my place for Christmas Eve."

"Where exactly is that?"

"My farm. I run a farm and live there, too. Between Radość and Milosna."

"A nice address."

"Let's take the Christmas tree from the steps. I have some emergency candles; we'll catch the last cab and then it's off to the country, peace and quiet, nature and truth. I have everything, a nice house, comfortable furniture, lots of money. There's just one little thing I'm missing—someone to share it all with."

"My wife is waiting for me."

"We'll find a way of sharing you. I don't make excessive demands anymore."

The streetlight bathed her in greenish light. Still a good-looking woman, she was holding the butt end of her life between clenched teeth. She was rich in bitter knowledge and melancholy resignation. The mature beauty which remained to her would have tempted more men than one. But, obviously, it was tempting no one.

"That's too far for me, Julia. It's too far to Radość and Milosna."

"I once made a very big mistake and I'm still living off

it. I married an American billionaire, I give you my word. Like a dumb Polish girl, I literally found the guy in the water, in the sea, at the beach. He wasn't old and he was rather good-looking. I was drowning and he tried to save me. I really was drowning, because I don't know how to swim. He was just wearing an ordinary bathing suit and so I didn't even know whom I was thanking for my life. Do you have any idea what eight hundred million dollars means? I'll just tell you that he had his own airline. When we'd fly to Europe in our jet, we would take our two favorite cars in the cargo hold. He was the fifth or sixth biggest taxpayer in the United States."

"And so?"

"And so nothing. He had a taste for whores and was a bit of a screwball. May the earth lie lightly on him. After a long life, of course. But he took care of me right. I bought myself the farm, never expecting that no one would come work there for me, for a lousy six thousand zlotys."

"Are you proposing that you and I bring the veal to town together?"

"We'll sow together, plow together, feed the cattle. We'll admire sunrises and sunsets together, be frightened by summer storms and suffer from insomnia together on long misty autumn nights. We could come to love each other."

"That's not for us. The escape I'm looking for is in the thick of things, the hurly-burly, people, the crowd. Twenty years ago I would have given your offer serious consideration."

"Twenty years ago you wouldn't have existed for me."

"You've skimmed through life, then."

"Oh yes, from top to bottom, or from bottom to top. Doesn't matter. Am I ugly?"

"No. You're nice-looking and clearly intelligent, you know how to be pleasant, and you will torture yourself right up to the very end like many good-looking wise women who jumped head first into the river, swallowed some water the wrong way, started to drown, and were pulled out onto shore . . . and were pulled out onto shore . . ."

"And what was on that shore?"

"That's just it. Nothing. Heaven and earth."

"Why don't we meet any people who succeeded in life?"

"We meet them all the time but we instinctively shun them like the plague."

"Does that mean positive heroes exist, Mr. Socialist-Realist?"

"They do. But not for you and me anymore."

"Duszek would say, When a Polish woman wants something, she'll even ditch her millionaire for it."

"A millionaire screwy from his millions."

"You don't need millions for that."

A municipal street cleaner came rolling down the middle of the street, out in the wrong weather. The entire city was buzzing with song like a soccer stadium or a Russian Orthodox heaven.

"How about it, Mr. K.?"

"We're of different bents. We wouldn't make it."

"You're worried about a few books. I've got money, we'll hire a ghostwriter who'll write a dozen bestsellers for you."

"Don't tempt me."

"You could fill a university with what I know about life, and I still have some of that Polish will to survive."

"You deserve a better guy."

"Excuse me, but please show me where those better guys are to be found. Poland was always a country of fine women and worthless men."

"You know what, I just split in two."

"What is that supposed to mean?"

"I flitted along the surface of life like you. The time to pay has come. No, not to pay, for what could I pay with? It's a little too late to choose. For I have perished already. You know, I dreamed of decadence on eschatological pillows. It was a rotten dream, as vexing as a nightmare, full of banal apparitions, vulgar terror, a dream not worth dreaming or hibernating through, if you prefer. And now, here, life, our fucked-up angelic life, is waking me again. Can I just pick myself up? I'd like to, but who with? And where to? And I'll tell you another secret—apparently I died last year at the beginning of June. At quarter to four in the morning at a certain bar. Who knows, it might have been the result of my troubles, that is, too much alcohol. So I committed suicide and I can't be alive, though life is now presenting me with the bill. I have to go back and start all over, but how can I do that if I'm dead?"

"Is there any sense in beating your head against the wall?"

"And if there was?"

An iced-over taxi drove up, its tires squealing on the fresh ice. It stopped right beside us, plowing into the high, snow-covered curb.

"It's a cab. Shall we take it?" asked Julia.

The taxi doors had opened before I could answer. The first to struggle out was a girl wearing a winter coat thrown over a robe, and some sort of slippers. Her face, however, had been made up rather festively. The next to emerge from the old-fashioned interior was a man with a bundled-up baby in his arms. At first we thought he must have gotten tanned dark as a black in Zakopane, but then we saw he really was a black, a young, energetic black, the infant's father.

"Give us a hand with this stuff, you guys," he said to

us, and fearlessly entered the hall of the building where we were camping out.

Kojran and I grabbed the collapsible baby carriage, the suitcase, and a bunch of plastic bags. Clearly the black man took good care of the woman who had just given birth.

We followed the new parents into the depths of the gateway, then through the courtyard and into that ruin which before the war had been a substantial outbuilding of a respectable apartment house. We climbed the wooden stairs, which reeked of urine, up to the first floor or the second, though in reality it was probably the fourth floor, the other two having been walled over.

We encountered a rather odd, makeshift arrangement —the corridor of a former apartment with its balcony torn off, some sort of door to what seemed to be drawing rooms and which had now become individual apartments. The black stood in front of the door decorated with a poster of a black singer. He shifted the bundled-up infant from one arm to the other, hunting for his apartment key.

"Shall we knock off half a liter?" he asked with a real Warsaw barroom accent.

"We're in a hurry to spend Christmas Eve at home," I said.

His wild eyes flashed, but he spoke like a Pole. "Spend Christmas Eve with us. Do you know what *slyzyki* are?"

"Of course," I said. "Cakes with honey water and poppy seeds."

"See, Zocha," said the black. "One of us."

"I know what *slyzyki* are, too," said Kojran.

"See, Zocha, another one. All right, then, let's get to it, you guys."

He opened the door and we saw a large room which looked like an Oriental seraglio. Ottomans, poufs, carpets, beads. Modernity was also represented in the plastic and nickel of stereo adapters and tape recorders. That black was either the son of Emperor Bokassa or traded currency in the Praga bazaars.

"We barely made it back here from the clinic. All right, then, throw that junk in the corner."

"The star of Bethlehem is shining. Could it be for your son?"

"Not for him. He was born a week ago. Come on, guys."

"Zdzisiek," said Zocha cautioningly.

"My dearest, we should have one glass at least."

"Zdzisiek, the gentlemen are in a hurry."

The black's spirit fell. To hide his confusion, he began diapering the child. We tiptoed back to the corridor under the anemic Zocha's icy gaze.

"He'll be all right," whispered Kojran. "He already knows what the hands of our girls are like."

A barely perceptible breeze was driving grains of snow along the corridor. There was no glass in the doors to the balcony. Someone had left the doors ajar and they beckoned invitingly out to the balcony, of which only the rusted rails remained. Carols could be heard in that war-torn house as well. Peace to men of good will.

"You see all those stars?" I asked Kojran.

"They're really shining, aren't they, though? It's been a long time since I've seen a sky like that."

"What do you think, was someone looking down at us from a flying saucer?"

"Who knows. Maybe there'll be something about it in the papers tomorrow."

"No chance of that. Only we saw them. And they us."

I walked up to the balcony and opened the paneless doors. There were two flights of empty space between me and the concrete covered with thin glassy ice. A Wartburg wrapped in rags of snow. A black cat ran zigzagging by in search of a familiar cellar window. Black cats used to signify bad luck. Nowadays they don't signify anything. Someone else has begun doing that now. It is something else that brings the bad luck now.

"An awful lot of stars," I whispered. "All of our people are up there somewhere, yours and mine, more souls up there than there are on earth. It's probably cold out there in that void. And the eternal ice. Not too encouraging. I don't like the cold. Or the dark."

"It's not cold at all. Take my word for it. No temperature at all. You wouldn't even notice, wouldn't even catch a cold, and that's a fact."

It was as bright as summer above the roof of the apartment building in front. The antenna of a streetcar, probably the last of the day, bent at the traction connection and sent off a shower of pale-blue electric flashes.

I took a step forward to stand on a slippery railing which jutted out over the courtyard like a black finger. I turned to Kojran. The biting cold was creeping up under my short sheepskin coat.

"Kojran, do I owe you something?"

"What do you owe me? Money, vodka, a kind word?"

"You don't remember. I owe you my life. I've been living on borrowed time. Borrowed from you."

"Leave me alone. Everything's turned around now. It might be better not to bring it all up. Do I know who's following me now?"

"No, Kojran, probably nothing perishes or dies. We impress ourselves in time like beetles in resin. Come here, you beetle, take two steps and give me a little push. You can see I barely have anything to stand on here, one puff and justice will be done."

"For what? You almost kicked off once already today.

It might happen again tomorrow or the next day. God knows the right time for you to go."

"That was just my neurosis. A neurosis of the heart. The unquiet of the heart. The rebellion of the heart. But I haven't been absolved. If I repent now, if I perform a lightning-swift act of contrition, swift and sudden as the memory of some unpleasantness from you, or from friends or from fate, if I quickly settle accounts with my fifty-year instant of life and you give me a push, thus executing a just sentence which weighs on me, I'll be saved in my downward flight just as I reach the ground. Look, Kojran, it doesn't happen too often that someone can discharge a cruel duty and make another person happy at the same time."

Kojran took a step forward but stopped just short of the doors. He grabbed on to the door frame with both hands as if to use those rotted planks to separate us.

"No, brother, I won't push you now. It was one thing then and now it's another. Jump yourself if you want to. All you have to do is lift your foot, hang in the air, and close your eyes."

"So, then, why did you follow me all those weeks and end up in prison because of me?"

Kojran was looking for a cigarette. He lit up and in the sudden flare of the cigarette's glow he looked young, as he must have looked once when he was Janek the musician or Lord Byron.

"You know what, Tadzek. The truth is that I wasn't trailing you with a sentence to execute. You passed sentence on yourself. Your every cell was afraid and running. As a careful reader I used your own themes to pep up waiting in line with a little intrigue. You decreed the sentence, you execute it."

"But it's you who's running away, Tadzek. Tomorrow

you'll get on an airplane and fly off to the next world, which is not the next world at all."

"Me, running away?"

"Sure, you're just drifting along the way you've drifted along all your life. Always farther from the epicenter. Or maybe it all stems from that unexecuted, forgotten sentence? Maybe part of it all stems from just that."

Kojran was dragging on his cigarette. A silver tooth I hadn't noticed before, a vulgar tooth, flashed in his mouth.

"Don't tempt me, Tadzek." I could feel the smile in his words.

"But I'm the sole witness to your running away. It's better to do away with the witness."

"Maybe I'm running away and maybe I'm not. If you want, we can toss this down the well of oblivion."

He showed me his shoulder bag through the opening where the glass had been.

"You'll just run down and retrieve it. So, then, do you pardon me?"

"Ah, what a faker you are. You twist and turn, but nothing comes of it. Why not make things simple, like regular people?"

"How like regular people?"

"You have to find out how yourself."

"All right, then. It's awfully late. What will I say when I get home?"

I went back into the corridor. A child's crying could be heard. Most likely the newborn mulatto. We went down the stairs holding on to walls disgusting as those in a latrine. Then we were back in the courtyard, the old ruin looming above it like a black lid. Someone was slowly coming our way, a tall, thickset man in a wet jacket. It was Duszek.

"When a Pole sees a balcony, he wants to jump," he said in a hoarse, bass voice.

"Let's beat it," said Kojran. "What the hell possessed me to waste a whole day. Where's my samovar?"

"It's still on the steps."

"And everybody?"

"Waiting."

"Waiting for what?"

"For you. They want to wish you a happy holiday."

We walked to the gateway, where the wind had died down. They were standing on the stair landing like frozen capsheaves.

"Want a cig?" The anarchist opened his small tin box.

"Go to hell. Julia, is there enough for a parting cup?"

Our peasant woman reached into her pack. "Maybe we should break the Christmas wafer first?"

We began breaking the white symbol of bread, which snapped apart with an indecently loud sound.

"Bon voyage, Tadzek, if your name is Tadzek."

"And you, Tadzek, goddamnit, remember, lift our spirits, you got that?"

The student was again translating a declaration by the anarchist, who was sticking an entire half wafer in under his red mustache. "He says he'll be here waiting with us."

"Here in the hall?"

"No, in general."

"And what is he waiting for?"

"What all people are waiting for."

Grzesio was rubbing his numbed hands. A black blood clot had dried under his nose.

"A stoolie with staying power," said Duszek forgivingly. "Looks like I'll be breaking the wafer with him. All right, then, come over here, you shitass."

"And what are you still doing here?" I asked the woman in the pelisse.

"I'm a widow. There's no one to go home to."

"So let's share the wafer, then, if you won't be offended by a religious superstition."

"Ah, once a year it's all right. On a night like this. You don't like me because I'm objective."

"No reproaches today. We'll start all that up again tomorrow."

"What will we start up again tomorrow?" asked the construction worker, still embracing Goska.

"We've got to start something."

The stars above us were leaving orbit. Gripped by ice and cold, the city was still crooning carols in a drowsy murmur. Peace to men of good will.

The student approached me, took me by the arm, and pulled me off to one side. "We're collecting money. Will you chip in?"

"For what?"

"For people."

"Which people?"

He brought his lips closer to my ear. I could feel the meager warmth of his breath on my cheek. "For those who fight for freedom."

A sudden shudder went through me. My back was wet through. I had caught a cold for the holidays. The terrible magic of those newspaper catchwords. There beneath the starry night they resonated piercingly into my bone marrow, no, into the deepest fiber of my heart.

"For your freedom and ours," I repeated with numbed lips.

He didn't respond. He just stood there and waited. Like a reproach of conscience.

"I've got some money. It was for the rings," I whispered, fumbling inside my coat. "What does anyone need rings for? They're a symbol of shackles."

I found my pocket, but it was empty. I turned it inside out and every which way.

"The money's not there. I lost it or somebody stole it. No money even for the gate. The gate to the prison of everyday life."

"Excuse me, then."

"Wait, I have a knickknack here from my family home." I pulled out that malachite seal and tried to give it to him, but he withdrew his hand from that fragment of foreign rock. He thought I was mocking him, making fun of his mission. "Take it. It's money, too. You could sell it for a good price in an antique store, the kind sentimental foreigners go to."

*

* *

It could have happened this way: Traugutt leisurely descended the traceried steps of the railway car. Without looking about, his skilled conspirator's eye was able to observe that the platform was practically empty. The station-master was standing near the locomotive asking the engineer some question. A tall, bearded porter was swaying sleepily in the station door beside a brass bell. A police patrol walked unhurriedly alongside the train—a young, elegant officer in a sky-blue uniform and two non-coms. Now they had seen Traugutt. And he had seen them, even though he was busy checking his old repeating watch against the station clock.

He set his bag down on the gravel platform and looked casually about for a porter. There were several standing behind the green fence which separated the station area from a street planted with young lindens. But none of the porters was in any hurry to aid the solitary traveler. They, too, were waiting.

Traugutt carefully replaced his watch in his vest pocket. At that moment the patrol came to a halt two paces in front of him. The officer saluted politely; with their cold-reddened hands the non-coms took hold of their large swords in leather scabbards.

"May I have your passport, please?" requested the officer.

"Yes, of course." Traugutt handed him a sheet of paper folded in four.

The gendarme read the document, peering closely with discreet curiosity at the traveler. The station porter struck the bell and shouted something in Volga Russian.

"Your name, please?" asked the officer, without lifting his eyes from the paper.

"Czarnecki."

"Yes, and your first name?"

"Michal."

"Merchant? Here on business?"

"Yes, on business. For one day."

"I suppose you'll be staying in the European Hotel?"

"If I can get a room."

"I hope you do. I wish you a good stay." The officer returned the document, saluting again.

Only then did a porter wearing a large sackcloth apron come running over. No doubt he was an Old Believer, a square-shouldered, unshaven peasant with a cheerless smile.

"Do you have cabs here?" asked Traugutt in Polish.

"All you want," answered the porter in a deep voice. "We got plenty of cabs, sir."

"Show me the way, then."

They walked out in front of the station accompanied by the discreet glance of the police officer. Tangled filaments flew through the golden air. Traugutt stopped and looked up at the milky sky, which he had not seen for months.

A cab galloped up. The porter set the bag beside the

feet of the young driver. Traugutt hurriedly wiped his
steamy glasses with the end of his scarf and then pulled
himself up onto the wobbly vehicle. The cabdriver turned
around for a moment and looked his passenger straight in
the eye. Traugutt did not return the glance, though he had
immediately noticed the driver's official number sewn inside out on his back, which, in certain provinces, was a
sign of belonging to the resistance.

"To the European," he said, looking into the depths of
the tapering street paved with reddish fieldstones.

"I know the town well." The driver lashed the fat
sides of his black horse with the reins. "If I could be of
any help . . ."

"Thank you. I'm just here for one day."

The driver turned around again, this time with a
watchful smile. "Perhaps you would like to make the acquaintance of some very elegant women. I know their
addresses. You can have a good time here. Merchants and
officers come here from Lodz, even Warsaw."

Traugutt avoided his gaze. He blinked his eyes behind
his glasses, for an icy wind had sprung up in the depths of
the street, driving a cloud of blood-red leaves along in
front of it.

"I haven't the time, friend. Perhaps some other time."

The driver gave up. He busied himself with his lazy
horse, which raised its tail and began to shower out green-
brown apples of dung. The town seemed to crouch, lurk-
ing in the last of the autumn sun over the west. Pedestrians
walked quickly without exchanging greetings. The policemen thumped their numbed arms on street corners, in
windows people's faces could be glimpsed half hidden by
curtains—they were waiting and had been waiting for
many months with a mixture of hope and despair.

Suddenly movement in the street. An officer on horse-
back, his saber bared, came racing down the middle of the

street. "Make way! Make way!" he shouted in an ear-splitting voice.

The driver immediately pulled over to the gutter and stopped his horse. An armed cavalcade flashed boisterously by—fifty Cossacks surrounding an open cart bearing an order-laden general reclining on a black tufted seat and beside him, standing stiffly, a young officer, most likely his adjutant.

"The governor general," the driver informed, and then added carefully, "A severe man."

"Yes, I see," said Traugutt indifferently.

It grew quiet again. People began to emerge from the doorways where they had found shelter. In some courtyard a peddler began wailing in praise of his wares. The north wind was blowing harder and harder. Traugutt decided to put up his overcoat collar lined with dark-blue velvet.

The cab stopped again. With his crop the driver pointed out a mist-covered square by the river where three tall, broken posts gleamed in the day's final light.

"The governor general is a severe man," repeated the driver.

It was only then that Traugutt spotted the three dark shapes turning in the wind by the posts. Gallows. Three gallows, like three crosses.

"Well, here we are," said the driver.

Traugutt recovered his senses after a momentary lapse. "How much will that be?"

"I leave that to you, sir."

As he walked into the hotel lobby, Traugutt noticed that the driver was not leaving but watching him as if waiting for something. A man wearing a cap walked over to the cab, the two men discussed something, and then the man with the cap hopped up onto the step of the cab, which set off at a trot back to the station.

A spy or a rebel? Traugutt asked himself.

Officers in field uniform were milling about the lobby. Some were running up the stairs to their rooms, some were running down ready to go out; others were sitting in worn leather armchairs pausing for a few minutes for good luck before a long journey. Behind the counter a short, bald, bearded man gazed inquiringly at Traugutt.

"I need a nice room for one night."

The bald man with the beard smiled knowingly. "The officers have grabbed all the best rooms. For one night, too."

Traugutt rustled a paper ruble shimmering like a rainbow. "Don't let me down, friend. We've already arranged to meet here. A delicate matter, you understand."

"I understand everything," said the desk clerk, tucking the ruble up his sleeve. "Perhaps I can find something suitable for you, sir. Only I must ask you for your passport, please; nowadays that's the most important thing, the passport." He winked ambiguously but, at the same time, merrily at his client.

He rummaged about in his register, his brows rising in surprise; he smiled again, more ambiguously this time, his hands made a zealous whisking motion, and finally he handed Traugutt a key weighted with an oak ball.

"Shall I register the woman or admit her directly?" he asked in a subdued voice.

"Admit her directly. Time is short."

"I see," chortled the bearded clerk. "In times like these nobody has a minute to waste. Vincenty, take the gentleman's bag."

The gray-haired porter looked at Traugutt with unfriendly curiosity, picked up his suitcase, and started up the stairs without a word. Still silent, he opened the door to the room, accepted his tip, and was about to leave in silence when Traugutt stopped him with a beckoning hand at the threshold. "You have good champagne?"

Vincenty shrugged his shoulders. "Good. The same as everywhere."

"Why are you so close-mouthed?"

"And why not? A person should be able to understand."

"Understand what, friend?"

"What will do, and what won't."

Traugutt thought for a moment, his coat in his hands. Suddenly the wind began yelping in the gutters, a bare tree bent over and looked in the window.

"All right. Order a bottle of champagne on ice. If you have ice."

"We have ice, why shouldn't we," grumbled Vincenty, and left, closing the door a bit too loudly.

Traugutt went over to the large mirror, which stood in the corner. He saw his reflection in the dull, dark glass—a thin, slight man wearing wire-framed eyeglasses. He sighed as if disappointed and smoothed the dark hair by his prominent ears. The wind tore at the window, the poorly puttied panes rattling slightly. Someone was walking around in the next room, taking large strides on the squeaking floor.

Traugutt went to the window, drew the dirty, gummy curtain aside, and shuddered again as he had before in the cab. Above the bare, feeble tree he saw that same view of the square—a streak of river and the white hooks of the gallows. The desk clerk had taken pains to give him a good room with a front view.

Traugutt closed the curtain tightly and then looked out in the corridor. "Vincenty!"

"What?" came a rheumy voice from below.

"Bring me a light."

A few men were talking in the next room. Traugutt listened for a moment to their muffled speech, which he then recognized as Russian.

Involuntarily he returned to the window and once again drew the curtain carefully. It was growing dark. The trees were being buffeted by gales of autumn wind; sparse dark clouds were flying southward like gigantic birds of prey. But now the gallows had been swallowed up by darkness. The square had merged with the gloom and all that could be seen were the outlines of the flower beds, their flowers withered in the premature autumn.

The door creaked. Vincenty carried in two zinc candlesticks, their flames struggling uncertainly. He set one down on the table and the other on the wobbly, dust-covered étagère. He then left and immediately returned carrying a damp pail, from which the neck of a greenish bottle protruded.

"What do you have for dinner?" asked Traugutt.

"What would you like? There might be some veal cutlets."

"That'll do fine."

Vincenty was still standing by the door.

"Is there something you want to say?"

"No. Nothing."

He sighed and left the room, the flames fluttering in the invisible draft. Traugutt took out his watch, glanced at it, and then tried to wind it with the little key, but it seemed already to be wound as far as it would go. He replaced his watch and walked over to his suitcase. He opened it, took out a bottle with a large glass stopper, poured a splash of transparent lotion onto his palm, and then rubbed his neck, temples, and hands. He was about to walk over to the mirror but changed his mind, waving his hand in a gesture of dismissal and, in doing so, smelled his hand. His neighbors had started rattling their tableware in the next room. A dinner was being prepared there as well.

Traugutt sat down on the frayed bedspread and

waited, prevailing over the long-drawn-out seconds and minutes. Guitar strings twanged in the next room. A fly which had escaped death during the first frost was loitering near the blackened stucco ceiling.

Traugutt stood up as if about to rush off somewhere, but then sat back down on the bed, rubbing his bony hands. Time barely seemed to move.

At last he heard a gentle knock. He sprang to the door, opening it in one violent motion. She was standing in darkness, but he immediately recognized the greenish eyes blazing like a cat's, the turned-up nose.

He swept her into the room and slammed the door shut. They fell into each other's arms, where they remained quite some time until they were composed.

"So, daughter of Kosciuszko, how's life, how's everything?"

She withdrew from his arms and lifted her delicate veil. She smiled uncertainly, ashamed.

"Perhaps we should sit down," said Traugutt, suppressing the trembling of his hands. "You'll be more comfortable in the chair. Or on the bed."

"No, here's fine." She sat down quickly on the wicker chair and hid her hands in her fur muff.

"I don't know where to begin, Tonia. How are things at home, the children?"

"Everything's the same at home. The children are growing. We worry about you. There hadn't been any news for such a long time."

"Everything will be all right now."

"All right how? Why aren't you coming back home?"

"The war, Tonia. I can't come back."

They looked greedily at each other as if they saw themselves for the first time. She saw his first gray hair, his glasses in which the two small candles glowed, his overwhelming commonness, and he saw her young face flushed from the cold, her turned-up nose inherited from her grand-uncle, and her full lips, which were all her own.

The door opened and Vincenty entered with their dinner. He set the food on the table, glanced disapprovingly in Tonia's direction, and left, closing the door behind him.

"Perhaps we should drink some champagne first?" asked Traugutt.

"Whatever you want," she whispered.

As he popped the cork, men burst into laughter in the next room.

"Are you out of danger?"

"Is anyone?" He raised his glass. "Do you know what I'm drinking to?"

"I know."

They dampened their lips, embarrassed by the impropriety of the hotel, the shouts from the next room, and that champagne. Somewhere in the city there was the distant blast of a shot absorbed immediately in a sudden howl of wind.

Traugutt rose and walked over to the woman. He embraced her awkwardly, which caused the veil to fall and again cover her face.

"Tonia, what's the matter?"

"This hotel makes me feel embarrassed."

"Me too. But what can we do. Perhaps you'd like to take off your coat."

She rose obediently and gave up her warm cloak, which smelled of heather. Something dark red shone in her hands. She caught his eye. "Give me your hand," she said.

She poured a handful of small, dark chestnuts into his hand.

"They're from Ostrow," she added. "Where will you be going?"

"To Warsaw. Aren't you hungry? The cutlets are getting cold."

"I don't feel like eating."

"Me either. Come over here, sit down on the bed. We have to whisper."

They sat on the high bed, their backs against the tall pillows, which smelled freshly ironed. Someone was playing deep, melancholy chords on a guitar in the next room.

"Why are you going to Warsaw?"

"I'm assuming the leadership of the People's Government."

"Why does it have to be you?"

"Why does it have to be me? Perhaps it's the will of God." The candle flames swayed drowsily like graveside memorial candles. The hotel's drunken night life had begun. Someone was running up the corridor, someone was shouting from down below, someone was pounding impatiently on a door. Amid all the clamor, the vicious autumn's ominous voice, filled with tragic determination, made itself heard from time to time.

"They say the uprising's dying out," she whispered.

"The situation is bad. But Poland will not die."

"Was there any sense in rising up against such force?"

"Is that you saying that, daughter of Kosciuszko?"

"Yes, it is."

"I don't know if there was any sense in it. I do know that it had to be done."

"Treacherous leaders, stupid politicians, the classes at odds with each other, an army of spies everywhere. Sometimes I have this terrible thought that the only reason the uprising continues is that it is supported by provocateurs from the Okhrana."

Traugutt said nothing. They could hear the sound of their breathing and the hubbub from the next room. The

guitar rang out again. Its speeded-up rhythm drew someone into song, and soon a timid, guttural tenor could be
heard singing:

> *Farewell, unwashed Russia.*
> *Land of slaves, land of masters.*
> *And to you, light-blue uniforms,*
> *And you, the nation which obeys them.*

Traugutt sought her small, hot hand.

"Yes, there is considerable suspicion that large numbers of agents and provocateurs have infiltrated the patriotic movement. Perhaps the line between a spontaneous
and a provoked action, a noble deed and a base one, has
been erased. So what to do then, hide in passive suspicion,
justify fatal inaction with a lot of noise about prudence?"

"The people must endure."

"But who can tell the difference between enduring
and agony?"

"I know, I know, my love. But my heart bleeds every
time I see young people being carted off to Siberia, when I
see the gallows with our murdered martyrs."

"There's probably no other way, Tonia. There's no
other way if we don't want to become abased and stunted,
and die held in contempt by other nations."

In the next room a few voices rose more boldly with
the second stanza of the song:

> *Perhaps beyond the Caucasus*
> *I can hide from your Pashas.*
> *From their all-seeing eyes,*
> *From their all-hearing ears.*

Tonia listened, her brow furrowed beneath a gar-
land of light hair. Her thin fingers tightened on her husband's hand. "Aren't those forbidden songs they're singing?" she whispered.

"They can do anything. Today they're singing, tomorrow they'll be hanging people."

"Aren't you tired? You have a long journey ahead of you."

"I can't be tired now. A terrible responsibility will rest on my shoulders."

"Do I feel you trembling?"

"It's the cold. I forgot to ask them to make us a fire."

"Let's cover ourselves with the quilt. But put the candles out first."

He blew out both candles and with trembling hands began removing his clothes beside the wicker chair. Out of the corner of his eye he saw Tonia struggling with her dress. He heard the glassy rustle of her petticoat. A cadaverous specter, the window seemed cut out of the darkness itself.

He ran barefoot across the freezing floor to the tall bed. Tonia was waiting, having turned down a corner of the quilt. They drew the quilt over their heads and began warming their little hideaway with their breath.

"Do you still remember me, Tonia?"

"Do you remember me?"

"I think of you all the time. Every night, every day."

"You forgot to take off your glasses."

"You're right."

Emerging from their warm nest, he placed his glasses on the floor.

"I felt awfully ashamed coming into the hotel alone."

"Receiving a young woman in my room makes me feel ashamed, too."

Timidly he lay his hand on her breast, which was covered by her thin chemise. She submitted tensely to this intimate gesture. With dry lips he kissed the lock of hair beside her burning ear. Just at that moment someone began knocking at the door.

"Didn't you lock it?" she whispered in alarm.

"No, I didn't."

He sprang from the bed, threw his coat over his shoulders, and opened the door. Vincenty stood in the corridor, a lamp in his hands.

"I've come to warn you, Mr. Czarnecki. Your passport is being kept at the police station," the old man said quietly, with no trace of his former animosity.

"They'll check it carefully, but it's good, a merchant passport. They'll return it tomorrow."

"If you wish to leave here secretly, I can help you."

"Thank you for your good will. I don't have to run away. I don't need to."

"As you see fit. But, just in case, I'll be down below."

The old man looked intently into Traugutt's eyes, trying to read the truth. Someone came running out of the next room and dashed headlong down the stairs.

"Well, good night, then."

"May God reward you," said Traugutt, turning the key in the lock.

He returned to the bed, where Tonia was waiting, sitting upright, tense, her arms crossed over her breast.

"People's boundless dedication. And it might all be in vain," he whispered and reached for his glasses, but they were on the floor, faintly reflecting the gray rectangle of the window.

She turned toward him, suddenly clinging to him, burying her face in the curve of his shoulder. He wanted to take her in his arms, but in that warm, cramped space, her chemise had been pulled up and suddenly he felt her young pulsing body in his hands. A sweet, swift panic seized him and his quivering lips began hastily kissing the hot skin of her rough, taut nipples, her damp sweat which smelled like herbs. She clasped her frail arms around his neck, let her eyelids close over her gleaming eyes, and waited, holding her breath. With a strange, desperate fear that might have seemed brutal, he forced his way blindly into her, aware of the terrible drumming of his own blood and had barely entered that spasmatic, painful heat when he was suddenly swept into a great alleviation such as he had never known before.

The stubborn buzzing of the fly near the ceiling could be heard again. Tonia lay motionless, waiting to no avail. She stared up at the ceiling with wide-open eyes, which contained the diminished shadows of the struggling trees in the wind-swept street.

"I haven't been with a woman for a long time," he whispered, despair in his voice.

"You haven't been with me for a long time, General." She smiled and turned to him.

Free now of desire, he began kissing her hot, moist lips and she returned his kisses with understanding restraint.

"Forgive me," he tried to whisper, but she would not let him, covering his mouth with her hand.

"We have the whole night before us."

"Yes, the whole night."

"And then you leave for Warsaw."

"Yes, Tonia, then I leave."

"But why does it have to be you?"

"It's my duty." He was about to add "as a man," but decided not to.

A wild and brutal uproar had arisen next door. Some-one was doing a Cossack dance, leaping and squatting, making the bamboo étagère respond with a monotonous trembling.

"Do you realize you're heading for certain death?" said Tonia suddenly.

"I want to avoid an untimely death like anyone else," he whispered after a moment's thought.

"If you stay at your post to the end, that's certain death."

"Someone has to die . . ."

". . . so that others may live." Tonia finished the phrase with a sneer.

"Who am I, Tonia? A nobody. Not handsome, not particularly gifted, of no great importance. I am an ordinary particle of our nation. I feel no pity for myself."

The sound of breaking glass rang out in the next room. Someone was howling at an unseen moon.

"They'll keep us awake."

"Tonia, what right would I have to safeguard my own life? How is it different from anyone else's?"

"What about me? And your children?"

"I don't know if I've given you happiness. If I've given you anything at all. I feel like a swindler."

She kissed him. He saw her face before him darkened by the night, the face of a Ruthenian madonna.

"You're being foolish, General."

Now they were smashing furniture next door. Someone was battering his head on a table to the accompaniment of hoarse laughter. Traugutt rose silently from the bed and began putting his coat on over his underclothing.

"Leave them alone. Better not to draw any attention to yourself," said Tonia.

"We couldn't last till morning like this. They're just getting started."

He went out to the corridor and knocked at the door of the next room. No one opened it, no one heard him knocking in all the drunken clamor. He pressed the handle and opened the door, revealing a large suite crammed with officers from all branches of the service, their shirts unbuttoned. He spotted at once the light-blue uniform of the police officer who had checked his passport at the station.

Traugutt, however, was not noticed immediately. One by one they stopped talking, turning their eyes toward the open door. Finally the room grew quiet, and the only sound was that of spilled water dripping monotonously in one corner.

"Excuse me, gentlemen, but my wife is ill. I'm asking you to be quiet because she cannot fall asleep."

A young captain rose from the table and in horror Traugutt recognized on his sapper's uniform the number of the same regiment in which he himself had served not long before.

"It is we who are to be excused, Mr. . . ." said the captain, clicking his heels.

"Czarnecki," said Traugutt, bowing.

"We have the honor, Mr. Czarnecki, of begging yours and your wife's pardon for this irregularity." He was standing at attention, reeling from side to side. "Let us find justification, yes, in the circumstance that this is our farewell, stag party, yes. Tomorrow we go out into the field, Mr. Czarnecki, and tomorrow, yes, at this hour, half of us may no longer be alive, yes."

"I understand, still . . ."

"It is I who understand, Mr. Czarnecki; we, his majesty's officers . . ."

"Forget it, Alyosha" said the police officer, looking at the bottom of his tall glass.

"Shhh, shhhh." The captain tottered toward Traugutt. "We wish Madame Czarnecki a good night, yes."

Traugutt returned to his room. Removing his coat, he said softly, "They are afraid of death, too."

He slipped back in under the quilt kept warm by Tonia's body.

"Will the police return your passport tomorrow?"

"Do you think fate will spare me? That they'll grab

me tomorrow and send me off to Siberia instead of hanging me in a month or a year? No, they'll return my passport and I will go to Warsaw to accept the role of dictator of a nonexistent state."

"Are you saying that bitterly?"

"I'm telling you what is, the way things have turned out."

The next room had quieted down. Only the floor creaked from time to time, or someone spoke loudly. The wind was lashing the old, leaky roofs.

"It must be winter already back home in Lithuania. You see the kind of weather they have here, rain and wind and that's it. Are you sleeping, Tonia?"

But he saw that she was staring up at the ceiling. He pulled her suddenly over to him. "I love you so much, Tonia. I'm so grateful to you."

"Why should you be grateful to me?"

Then he sought out the edge of her chemise, embraced her young hips like sheaves of fresh rye, and began ardently kissing her pulsing neck, her frail neck, which smelled of his forgotten home, distant Ostrow, safety lost. He felt desire return to him and he gathered her beneath him; she submitted with bashful passivity, though she was full of humiliating expectation.

Now his desire was great, arousing a tender spirit in him; he pressed hard on her breasts with his trembling fingers. She gasped with pain, he crushed her with his weight, then faded, for that shallow desire had already melted away into sleepy languor and dulled resignation. He lay on top of her and in despair tried to collect himself. From outside came the succulent clopping of hoofs on a cobblestone street. A Cossack patrol dashing out of darkness back into darkness.

"My hand's asleep," complained Tonia.

He realized that she was trying to defuse the situa-

202

tion. He kissed her once again in gratitude and fell back on the large pillow beside her.

"A bad time for a meeting," she whispered. "But maybe it'll all pass and you'll come back home to Lithuania."

"Tonia, I want to come back, I just may not be able to."

She covered her slender shoulders. She lay there a long time, and Traugutt thought that she must have fallen asleep. But the curl of hair by her ear shook with a barely perceptible spasm like a goldfinch feather.

"Are you crying, Kosciuszko's daughter?" he asked, his heart grieving.

"It's nothing, nothing," she murmured, burying her face in the pillow. "Women have to weep sometimes."

A great shout broke the silence outside. "Help! Help!"

Police whistles rang out, people began running back and forth in front of the hotel. Tonia sat up, covering herself with one corner of the quilt.

"You hear that?"

"The war's still going on, Tonia."

"Yes, they're chasing someone, some nameless man."

"Nameless men have always won their freedom by fighting for it. The names of the heroes are preserved to give us memory and courage, but always, at every moment, good or bad, every time the earth turns, some nameless man is biting off his handcuffs with his own teeth."

"Look, day is breaking," she said softly.

The window was slowly growing lighter. The wind had died down as if in expectation of the day, one more short autumn day in that ominous year.

I must get up and meet my death, murmured Traugutt to himself.

She was about to ask her husband what he was saying, but then, in sudden horror-filled foreboding, she

203

stopped herself and froze, her hand reaching timidly toward his face, which still bore the impress of his wire-framed glasses. It could have happened like that.

.*

*   *

We walked along a sidewalk covered with pieces of broken glass which crackled like December ice. We listened to the silence of the dead city. There was a large uncommonly clear moon over the apiary of the ruins. You could see mountains and valleys on the moon, the rubble and canyons made by nonexistent rivers. You could also see paths worn by the astronauts and their excrement frozen for all eternity.

I was carrying a heavy bundle wrapped in sackcloth on my back. Julia was trotting along beside me, and now she was once again an old woman whose sons had been killed. The rest of the refugees were trailing along behind us. Kojran was carrying his booty, a samovar. He had found it in some collector's apartment or on the shore of a river that smelled of corpses. Duszek blew on his numbed hands as he walked. He had only a bit of life left ahead of him. He would not have to make many more choices. Goska and the construction worker were holding hands. They had lost their families and would begin life anew, in the basement of a burned-down house. The woman in the voluminous pelisse would not perish because she had a purse full of jewels under that pelisse. The student was coughing; the frost was aggravating an old gunshot wound in his lung. The student was guiding the blind anarchist, whose eyes had been gouged out in a concentration camp. Last came Grzesio, looming like a specter, a rope around his neck. We were all there.

"Didn't I tell you?" groaned the woman in the pelisse. "I always warned you."

"We'll begin anew," I said.

"We know how to begin anew," added Kojran. "God's taught us that."

"But what about our sins?" asked Duszek, catching up. "What about that black cloud of sins, Mr. K.?"

We were in front of the jewelry store, the display windows black, grimy pits. The blind neon. Semi-precious stones from the Urals were scattered gleaming by the wall. Like slag from uranium ore.

"And how can I begin again?" asked Grzesio plaintively.

There was a trolley car lying across the street. As in a mirror the entire moon was contained in one fragment of one pane of glass. A dead portrait of a dead satellite.

"How about me?" repeated Grzesio.

"We'll begin with forgiveness," said Kojran. "I forgive you who, for several of the best years of my youth, I trailed with a death sentence."

The broken torso of a hotel which once reached the clouds. An execution wall recently riddled by bullets, a smashed lamp with an eternal flame in front of the memorial wall. But someone's hand had already kindled a flame on the Christmas-tree candle. That drop of red, barely alive, warmed memory as it rose from the dead.

"Do you hear?" repeated Kojran. "I forgive and I ask forgiveness."

"I hear," I answered. "I ask forgiveness of you all."

"Where are we going now?" asked the woman in the pelisse.

"To our own lives."

"From the beginning."

"One more time."

The Palace of Culture, an extinguished torch, rose to

the sky. Cracked like the burnt-out stump of an old oak. Shaken by the many explosions which were to crumble it. White soot was again drifting through the air. And up above, the tin sheet of the firmament riddled with holes and particles of mysterious light which gave neither heat nor illumination.

"We will sow other grain."

"We will plant other trees."

"We will build other cities just like this one."

"Happy holidays, Robinson Crusoes."

"Happy holidays, free Robinson Crusoes."

"Happy holidays of freedom."

"Happy holidays of another freedom just like this."

They walked away in all directions from this crossroads of broad avenues which was and is the navel of the world, our world. They disappeared in the black, infernal shadows of the death which will be the beginning of a new life.

"How's it going?" asked Julia. "Is my bundle too heavy for you?"

She was fixing her makeup by the light of that degenerate moon, squinting at the little mirror in her compact. She was a tough modern girl going on forty, with the face of a madonna and the personality of a truck driver. The Christmas tree at the rotary stood straight and tall, at rest, shining with the few bulbs that had survived. Isolated, ragged flakes of snow or hoarfrost fell slowly from the serene sky,

"Look, the city seems dead."

"That's because it's quiet," whispered Julia. "And the light is ghostly. A fatal night for lunatics."

"For you and me."

"For everybody."

"There's no more stars, no more unidentified flying objects."

"Yes, they flew off."

"At what moment in time did they see us?"

"Did they see us at all? And, if they did, did they understand?"

"But it's always encouraging to think that someone from out there saw us."

Red navigation lamps were flashing on the Palace of Culture. Lights were on in a few windows. Most likely custodians dozing off over a cup of cold tea or saying their prayers. An empty tram was running south to north, rumbling like a peasant wagon.

"Let's walk by the hotel," said Julia. "It's easier to catch a taxi there."

We crossed the roadway, slipping on the ice. Everything was at a standstill in the towering hotel, too. On the roof a green neon sign flared and darkened in a monotonous rhythm.

"Well, how about it, coming with me to Radość?" asked Julia.

"But you know I won't go anywhere; there's no place left worth my going to."

"You got out of the game fast enough. What have you got left?"

"A blank sheet of paper and insomnia."

"Too bad, then."

"Julia, I'm tired of pretending. Pretending to be a man, a writer, a lover. Feigning feelings, fondness, passion. God created me more or less in his image. I'm in league with other people like myself. They're waiting for me because they need me."

"But really, that one obsession of yours is killing you."

"Yes, it is, and I'm amazed at myself. It keeps me bound to the earth. I want to tear free and fly off into boundless space, which I would like to acknowledge as my true fatherland, but I can't because I'm bound to this earth, goddamnit."

"No, that's not so. There goes something."

"Probably an ambulance."

"Perfect for me."

Julia went out into the street and stepped out in front of an ambulance skidding toward a bridge. The vehicle came to a halt, its siren stopped, and the driver, who looked like an old rustic squire, leaned out of the window, saying, "What's the matter?"

"Can you give me a lift to Radość?"

"Hell, it's not on my way."

"I'll make it worth your while."

"All right, but I'm in a hurry."

"I see and I appreciate it."

The driver hesitated and glanced over at someone hidden in the shadows of the cab. "Can't leave a girl out in the freezing cold," he said with a sigh. "We'll go a little out of our way. Climb in the back, you'll be more comfortable there."

I opened the rear doors of the ambulance and placed the bundle beside a stretcher on which a handsome Christmas tree lay trussed up like a madman.

"See you again in one line or another, for there's going to be more and more of them in this world," said the peasant woman from Radość.

"Farewell, Julia. Merry Christmas."

"Ah, goddamnit, wouldn't we have been good together?"

"It's good just the way it is, goddamnit, and it may be better yet."

"Merry Christmas, Mr. Konwicki."

The tires spun on the ice, aquamarine from neon, the ambulance squealed away and flew off toward Praga, howling like a wolf. The rotary was flooded in dead moonlight and deep shadows like those in a burned-down building. I walked up onto the rotary without knowing why myself.

"Basia!" I cried for no reason at all, startled by my own cry.

No echo came back from the city. The city devours all echoes.

"Iwona!"

A terrible, rural calm. Snow, ice, stars.

"Basia!"

Some new light struck my eyes. A truck I couldn't see was turning on its searchlight. A policeman stuck his head out from under a tarp and said, "Shut your trap or I'll come down there!"

Not wishing to trouble the policeman, I cut across the street into the shadows thrown by the clifflike department stores. But still I had some sort of idiotic hope that a girl would come running out from one of the apartment buildings with a coat thrown hurriedly over her or a warm housecoat smelling of lavender, camomile, or, best of all, gillyflower. Why do I still have such hopes, and will I go on cherishing them until my unknown end? There's something basically infantile about us humans. We are still a young species.

There was feverish activity on the other side of the street obscured by the darkness. In that cocoon of darkness a good-sized group was busily lifting some sort of openwork structure made of pipes. Beneath that structure lay gigantic white squares ready to be hung, bearing the dismembered inscription MOSCOW DAYS IN WARSAW. So, even Moscow was coming to visit us?

I rushed over to those people I had encountered in that snowy wasteland. They had begun welding the pipes together, perhaps to keep warm or for practice; they were spewing sparks in all directions as they adjusted their tools, which reminded me of flamethrowers. I singled out the oldest one, the sort who knows life. He shot me a furtive glance and turned up the burner. A great stream of red-blue flame cut through the ice like butter. And I, after all, am warmer than ice.

I walked up to him, lifted my slouch cap, a hand-me-down from my brother-in-law. "Sorry to bother you."

The foreman squinted suspiciously. "What is it?"

"Would you be good enough to give me a good fucking blast with that machine gun of yours?"

"What are you talking about? I don't understand."

"You giving me a burst of that holiday flame and oxidizing me once and for all."

"Get out of here, you pig. You drank too much with your Christmas wafer and now you're looking for happiness."

"No, that's not it, either. I can live without it. Merry Christmas."

"Beat it!"

He was right. The rightness of indestructible instinct. One must live. There is some sense to all this senselessness.

A straggling file of tipsy tourists was walking along in front of the department stores, returning to their hotel after a holiday dinner. They were holding one another's arms, wavering from side to side, as if performing a Tyrolean waltz, and singing: *"Heilige Nacht, stille Nacht."*

They haven't lost their appetite for Poland. They're waiting their turn in line.

They stopped in front of a shop window stuffed with lifeless plastic girls and boys, motionless as the angels on tombstones. One of the tourists began yodeling. They set off to cover the short distance to their hospitable hotel, built on a spot where executions had once taken place.

Hold it, where was it I was going back to? The Wilno

Colony, to my home, where I'll die, or perhaps to that valley which I invented as a sovereign, independent sanctuary in the midst of daily life?

Trembling seized me, and again I felt sweat on my back. An awesome amount of stars. Indifferent. Of no use to anyone. An awesome amount of sky accustomed to the sight of us. An awesome amount of God, the great judge waiting for the trial.

And then I said, "When a Pole flies into a fury, then woe to blind, slothful, venal Europe."

Before me the great massif of a crouching city. A silent fortress. Caves full of sleeping knights. Up above, a red glow like the breath of that city. That redness whirls along an invisible spiral and turns into indecipherable visions like the reflection of the depths of a calm ocean, the calm ocean of time. And I do not know whether that shape is a gigantic star, the image of a weeping woman, or the mouth of hell.

DALKEY ARCHIVE PAPERBACKS

Visit our website at www.cas.ilstu.edu/english/dalkey/dalkey.html

DALKEY ARCHIVE PAPERBACKS

CAROLE MASO, *AVA.*

HARRY MATHEWS, *20 Lines a Day.*
  Cigarettes.
  The Conversions.
  The Journalist.
  Tlooth.

JOSEPH MCELROY, *Women and Men.*

ROBERT L. MCLAUGHLIN, ED., *Innovations: An Anthology of Modern & Contemporary Fiction.*

JAMES MERRILL, *The (Diblos) Notebook.*

STEVEN MILLHAUSER, *The Barnum Museum.*
  In the Penny Arcade.

OLIVE MOORE, *Spleen.*

STEVEN MOORE, *Ronald Firbank: An Annotated Bibliography.*

NICHOLAS MOSLEY, *Accident.*
  Assassins.
  Children of Darkness and Light.
  Impossible Object.
  Judith.
  Natalie Natalia.

WARREN F. MOTTE, JR., *Oulipo.*

YVES NAVARRE, *Our Share of Time.*

WILFRIDO D. NOLLEDO, *But for the Lovers.*

FLANN O'BRIEN, *At Swim-Two-Birds.*
  The Dalkey Archive.
  The Hard Life.
  The Poor Mouth.

FERNANDO DEL PASO, *Palinuro of Mexico.*

RAYMOND QUENEAU, *The Last Days.*
  Pierrot Mon Ami.

REYOUNG, *Unbabbling.*

JULIÁN RÍOS, *Poundemonium.*

JACQUES ROUBAUD,
  The Great Fire of London.
  The Plurality of Worlds of Lewis.
  The Princess Hoppy.

LEON S. ROUDIEZ, *French Fiction Revisited.*

SEVERO SARDUY, *Cobra* and *Maitreya.*

ARNO SCHMIDT, *Collected Stories.*
  Nobodaddy's Children.

JUNE AKERS SEESE,
  Is This What Other Women Feel Too?
  What Waiting Really Means.

VIKTOR SHKLOVSKY, *Theory of Prose.*

JOSEF SKVORECKY, *The Engineer of Human Souls.*

CLAUDE SIMON, *The Invitation.*

GILBERT SORRENTINO, *Aberration of Starlight.*
  Imaginative Qualities of Actual Things.
  Mulligan Stew.
  Pack of Lies.
  The Sky Changes.
  Splendide-Hôtel.
  Steelwork.
  Under the Shadow.

W. M. SPACKMAN, *The Complete Fiction.*

GERTRUDE STEIN, *The Making of Americans.*
  A Novel of Thank You.

ALEXANDER THEROUX, *The Lollipop Trollops.*

ESTHER TUSQUETS, *Stranded.*

LUISA VALENZUELA, *He Who Searches.*

PAUL WEST,
  Words for a Deaf Daughter and *Gala.*

CURTIS WHITE,
  Memories of My Father Watching TV.
  Monstrous Possibility.

DIANE WILLIAMS, *Excitability: Selected Stories.*

DOUGLAS WOOLF, *Wall to Wall.*

PHILIP WYLIE, *Generation of Vipers.*

MARGUERITE YOUNG, *Angel in the Forest.*
  Miss MacIntosh, My Darling.

LOUIS ZUKOFSKY, *Collected Fiction.*

SCOTT ZWIREN, *God Head.*

Visit our website at www.cas.ilstu.edu/english/dalkey/dalkey.html

Dalkey Archive Press
ISU Campus Box 4241, Normal, IL 61790–4241
fax (309) 438–7422